ABYSMAL

CANYON

BOOK ONE OF DOMINA LUMEN

M. E. NEIDHARDT

*To Peter & family —
Hope you enjoy!
Love, Eve*

Cover and interior title fonts designed by Manfred Klein

Printed by CreateSpace, an Amazon.com Company
Available on Kindle and other devices

To Frances and Dave for believing.

To the world of the unseen for inspiration.

Dowser - a person who uses a type of divination in attempts to forecast the future, diagnose ailments, locate ground water, buried metals, gemstones, oil, gravesites and other objects, as well as currents of earth radiation known as Ley Lines or energy lines, without the use of scientific apparatus. A dowsing rod or witching rod is sometimes used as well as a pendulum, although some dowsers use no equipment at all.

"What is soundless, touchless, formless, imperishable,

Likewise tasteless, constant, odourless,

Without beginning, without end, higher than the great, stable-

By discerning That, one is liberated from the mouth of death."

—the Upanishads

Contents

1. ABYSMAL

I lay in my sleeping bag listening to the sound of blood dripping on my tent. The heavy drops hit the top of the domed nylon like a drum in slow steady beats. For the past ten mornings the blood had become my macabre alarm clock, always occurring at the first light of dawn. The source was a Red Tail hawk perched above my tent in a pinion pine ripping chunks of meat from his daily prey.

My grandmother Oma said the blood was an omen. She believed my family was in grave danger at our secluded camp near the canyon rim. When I dowsed, my pendulum had confirmed her suspicions every day this week with a yes response, but nothing bad had happened yet. This was our last day of vacation and the morning of our annual family ritual. I refused to believe anything could go wrong on this day of all days at Abysmal Canyon, Colorado.

The date was June 21, 2025 and I was eighteen. It was the Summer Solstice, the day my family celebrated the marriage of Heaven and Earth, the Spirit of Life and the Source of All. My parents, older brother Dan, Oma and I came to the canyon every year at this time to renew our connection as a family of dowsers. Tomorrow we would drive home to Texas, but on this last morning, we would hike to the edge of one of the steepest canyons in North America and celebrate just as we had every summer since I was born.

In less than two months I would come back to this area to start as a freshman at Abysmal College. I couldn't wait to be free. My mom and dad loved me and I loved them, but they were just as ready for me to leave the nest as I was. The only down side to college that I could imagine would be living in the dorm with a roommate. I was used to being alone and I liked my solitude.

Dan and I grew up in an old two-story house on the edge of a rural community with no neighbors. Our parents preferred the privacy for their outdoor rituals. Because we were different, the town's people didn't understand us. They stayed away out of fear or respect and consequently, we had few playmates. I was convinced that sharing my private life at college with a stranger in one tiny room was going to be like fingernails on a chalk board every single day. But in return for that torture, I knew I would have my freedom to do whatever I chose and that made it all worth the sacrifice.

I sat up and inhaled a deep breath, filling my lungs with the fresh scents of spruce and sage. In the distance, I could hear the trailing screeches of Peregrine falcons echoing deep within the canyon. Their voices drifted down the black jagged walls into the narrow abyss then rose swiftly with the strong updrafts. I imagined flying with them with delta-shaped wings pointed backwards and feathers slick like sheer metal. We slipped in and out of the shadows between the passes then dove to the rushing waters of the Dragon's Tongue River and soared upward like arrows into the cerulean sky.

A rustling of footsteps just outside my tent brought me back to reality. They suddenly stopped.

"Morning' Ysolde." It was my father. His voice was strong and light.

"Mornin, Dad," I replied loud enough so he could hear me from inside the tent. I hastily pulled on my jeans and t-shirt.

"How'd my nature girl sleep?"

"Like a rock," I lied. Last night I couldn't stop thinking about Oma's premonition, but there was no way I was going to tell Mom or Dad and ruin this perfect day. I tugged on my hiking boots.

"I see your hawk friend is still here."

I pulled my long blonde hair back into a pony tail then unzipped the tent flap and peeked out.

Dad cast his gaze at the blood dripping down the side and raised an eyebrow.

"I'm going to miss him when we leave," I said.

"Will you miss the blood?" he grinned.

"That I can do without," I grinned back. "How's Oma this morning?"

"She's in the woods near Dan's tent talking to herself. I'm afraid her years of coming with us to the canyon are numbered." His eyes softened.

We exchanged a warm look for a moment. Oma was ninety-two. She was Mom's mother, but Dad loved her just as much, even though she was the most eccentric of the family. She believed electromagnetic energy was evil and lived underground without electricity in the field behind our house. She made money by dowsing for water wells, lost items, bad energy in homes and the occasional healing.

"We'll be heading to the rim shortly. Don't want to miss the sunrise on this day of days," Dad said, as he turned and walked back toward Mom.

"I'll be there in a sec." I sat back on my sleeping bag and reached behind my neck to unclasp the crystal pendant Oma had given to me when I was a child.

I held the pendant's chain between two fingers. The clear, hexagonal quartz hung patiently waiting my inquiry. I took a few breaths and tried to silence my mind then asked the same question I had asked for the past ten days.

"Is our family in grave danger here at the canyon?"

The crystal began to rotate clockwise. A yes response, just as it had responded every day this week. My heart sank. I wanted to trust my pendulum, but I refused to accept this answer.

"Will the danger occur today?"

The crystal swung clockwise again, this time with a swifter rotation.

"Stop! You're wrong! I don't know why I bother asking you anything."

4

The pendant stopped rotating and hung still like a scolded child. I stared at it for a moment. Sometimes pendulums changed their signals. It was a good practice to ask the pendulum to demonstrate what its yes and no responses looked like before each session. All week I had assumed the yes response was clockwise. Maybe I was wrong, maybe clockwise was a no response now.

I took another deep breath and asked the crystal to verify its answer.

"Show me a yes."

I watched the crystal closely, trying to keep my mind clear so I wouldn't influence the outcome. But, my inner voice was screaming for the pendulum to swing counter clockwise, proving what used to mean yes, now meant no. The pendulum swung back and forth a few times then slowly began rotating clockwise, just like before.

"Dammit," I sighed.

There was no way we were in danger. The weather forecast was for a beautiful day. Everyone seemed healthy and in good spirits. We were secluded and far away from anyone who might do us harm. The only explanation left was my lack of dowsing skills, which were poor at best. If a dowser can clear her mind of all thoughts and emotions, her pendulum should give an accurate reading. Throughout my training with Oma, I had failed miserably in that department. Oma could dowse correctly nearly 100% of the time. I was lucky to get half that.

I must be the reason for the inaccurate responses concerning today. At least that's what I was going to tell myself until we were all safely nestled back in our tents tonight.

My brother Dan popped his head inside the tent, startling me. My hand jerked and I dropped the crystal.

"Wake up, lazy bones!" he said with a big grin.

"You scared the crap out of me!" I laughed.

He saw the crystal lying on the sleeping bag. "Were you dowsing?"

"A little."

"Don't tell me you still believe Oma's prediction of doom and gloom."

"I'm trying not to, but the pendulum keeps saying yes."

"What does your gut tell you?"

"That everything's going to be fine."

"There ya go. Trust that feeling. Now come on, everyone's waiting."

Dan was the only one in the family who didn't dowse. It was a ridiculous waste of time in his opinion. Even so, he never missed the ritual at the canyon.

"Just one more question." I held the pendulum in front of me again.

"You can do that after the ritual." Dan playfully tried to yank it away.

"Hey!" I jerked it out of his reach.

"Then *come on.*"

"Okay, okay. But what if something horrible *does* happen?" I clasped the crystal back around my neck and exited the tent.

"Stop worrying. This is supposed to be a happy day, remember?" He made a goofy face.

"I guess you're right. And since when is my dowsing correct, anyway?"

"Exactly." Dan looked at the flies circling the dried bloody crust on the top of my tent. "That's so gross."

"Yeah, it is, but I kind of like it."

"And that's why you don't have a boyfriend," he chuckled.

"I know there's a guy out there somewhere who's just like me," I smiled.

"God forbid, two of you?" Dan laughed. "You do realize this is probably our last day together until Thanksgiving."

"I hate that," I said.

Dan had just turned twenty. He had driven from west Texas to meet us here at the canyon. He worked as a mechanic at a wind farm. I missed having him around. Now the main time we visited was during online gaming on the weekends.

"You'll be okay," he said. "You're going to college. That's pretty sweet. My little sis is gonna be a freshman." He reached toward my head to mess up my hair, but I dodged just in time.

"I'm pretty excited about leaving."

"You should be, Ysolde. I'm a little jealous."

"You? Jealous? You never wanted to go to college."

"I know. But, I bet the parties are kick ass!"

Dan loved to party, which was why he barely made it through high school. He was cute and popular with all the girls. No one could resist his charm.

"You can visit anytime and we'll check out the campus for wild and crazy times, how's that?"

"Only if I can stay in the dorm with you and all your girlfriends," he smiled.

"You're never going to change," I grinned, shaking my head.

"Never!" he shouted to the world. That was my bro. Full of life without a care, but still with a deep sense of loyalty to family.

"Let's go, Romeo."

I hooked my arm around his and we strutted across the campsite toward Mom, Dad and Oma waiting by the trail. Mom smiled at me then her brow wrinkled and her mouth tightened. I knew that look.

"Get your jacket, Ysolde. Remember how windy it is on the rim?"

"I'll be fine, Mom. Dan's not wearing one."

"Dan's different. Get your jacket," she insisted with a strict tone. I looked at Dad.

"It's not a bad idea, Ysy." I knew he was saying that just to appease Mom.

"Fine," I sighed.

Arguing was futile. I jogged back to my tent and grabbed my jeans jacket then walked over to Oma. She was tightly gripping her antique cane made of twisted wood. Her face was deep in thought.

"Good morning," I said gently.

Oma stood silently gazing down at the ground. She was deaf in one ear.

"Oma?" I said a little louder, touching her arm.

"Leave me alone!" she said sternly. She jerked her arm away from me.

"I'm sorry. I didn't mean to bother . . ."

"Go away! Leave my family in peace!" She yelled back toward the woods, raising her cane and shaking it in defiance.

I quickly scanned the area for an intruder to our little sanctuary, but saw nothing out of the ordinary.

"Who are you talking to?"

Oma's face turned toward me. Her eyes slowly focused as if emerging from a trance.

"Oh, good morning, dear," she said in her normal soft voice.

"Are you okay?"

She hesitated for a moment. "I'm not sure. I've been feeling a negative presence this morning. Something I haven't felt for a long time."

"Was it one of your visions?"

"It wasn't a vision. It was something else. Hopefully it will pass. Probably just old age, you know." She chuckled nervously, staring back into the woods.

"I dowsed this morning about today, but I must have done something wrong," I said.

"Did you clear your mind?"

"I tried, but you know how hard that is for me. The crystal keeps agreeing with your prediction. Everything's going to be okay, isn't it?"

Oma's lips tightened. "Don't worry, Ysolde. I won't let anything happen on this day of days."

Dan walked over to us. "Ya'll look *way* too serious. Ready to go to the rim, Oma?"

Oma straightened up a little and smiled at him. "Yes, I wouldn't miss it for the world, Danny." She looked at me with a sparkle in her eye. "We'll talk later," she whispered.

Dad tossed a daypack over his shoulder. "Let's go!"

We all started down the narrow dirt trail winding through the pines, junipers and black granite boulders. Canyon wrens darted about in the lavender pre-dawn sky. A sweet, cool breeze brushed across my cheeks. I watched from behind as Mom and Dad held hands. Mom's shoulder-length blonde hair waved gently back and forth. She turned her head to look back at me and Oma.

"Isn't it a beautiful morning? Just perfect," she said.

"Yes," I smiled. *Maybe too perfect*, I thought.

Oma squeezed my hand. She and I always walked together for the ritual. Her fingers were bony and cool, feeling more skeletal every year. I glanced down at her aged face. Her grey eyes were still bright and insightful. She had pulled her long white hair back in a braid and was wearing one of her simple, medieval-looking homemade dresses. The ragged hem drug along the ground collecting dirt, leaves and bits of nature. A soft black shawl she had knitted hung loosely from her bent back and narrow shoulders.

Dan brought up the rear. He was strong and tall and liked being in a position where he could see what was ahead and behind. This was always his place. Even as a child, he had been brave and adventurous. I felt safe knowing he was nearby.

After we had hiked a few hundred feet, Oma suddenly stopped. She immediately drew her hand away from mine and plunged it into her pocket, pulling out the familiar black stone I had seen her carry as long as I could remember. She held the stone in her palm and began rubbing it briskly between her thumb and forefinger.

"What's wrong?" I asked.

"Did you feel that?" she whispered, bending toward me, pulling her shawl over her head as if trying to hide.

I leaned close to her face. "Feel what?"

Dan caught up with us. "Hey, why'd you guys stop?"

"We're taking a short break," I said.

"A break? We just got started!"

"Oma needs to catch her breath. You go ahead."

"Don't take too long. The sun is about to rise."

"We won't."

Dan passed us and continued down the trail. I leaned in close to Oma's fragile, trembling body. "Now, tell me what you felt."

"I felt *him*. The same one I felt this morning."

"Him?"

"A flood of cold energy ran through my bones, numbing my muscles and piercing my heart. There's only one being who can do that to me." Her voice was shaking.

I scanned the forest again. "I still don't see anyone."

"He is here. He has somehow found a way through the Veil past the Great Pendulum."

"The what?"

"He can only be here for one thing. We have to catch up to the others to warn them."

"Warn them? What's going on?"

"Kraegon! A Vapor from another world! He has come to kill me, Ysolde! He will kill all of you in order to get to me. You must help me feel for negative energies just the way I taught you."

"*Kill* you? This is crazy, Oma."

"There's no time to explain. We must hurry to the others!" Oma began heading down the trail in a pace that was too quick for her frail body. I had never seen her walk with such urgency. I rushed to catch up with her.

The sky had begun to change to gray. Storm clouds were developing in the distance. The woods became engulfed in silence as if the trees were holding their breath, waiting for something dreadful to pass.

A large shadowy form suddenly flew across the trail directly in front of us. We both stopped. The air became icy. Oma began to shiver violently. I put my arm around her and then I felt strange, as if I were standing in the middle of two opposing forces warping back and forth.

"Whoa. I'm really dizzy. What's going on?" I took my arm away from Oma and stumbled sideways for a moment. "I think I'm going to be sick." I put my hands on my knees and took deep breaths.

"He's watching us. His powers are strong," she said, searching the treetops. Then her pale, fearful expression suddenly changed to happiness, filling her face with light and joy.

"Oh, my dear old friend, it's been such a long time. I'm so glad you're here. Yes, I know. We must leave at once." Her voice was calm and cheerful.

I was too sick to look up at the sky.

"Is it Kraegon?" I was totally confused. I didn't know if my granny had finally gone nuts, I was coming down with the flu or what was going on.

"Heaven's no, dear. That was Von."

"Who the hell is Von and why can't I see him?" I tried to stand upright without feeling nauseous.

"There's no time to explain. Are you wearing the crystal I gave you?"

"Always." I touched the pendant for reassurance.

"That will help protect you. Let's get the others before it's too late!"

A strong, menacing wind whirled around us. Lightning flashed on the other side of the canyon. We could see the others at the overlook. Dad had his arm around Mom. They were both facing us with their backs just a few yards from the mouth of the steep black chasm.

Dad motioned for us to hurry up. "Where have you all been? The sun is coming up!"

He seemed oblivious to what Oma and I had been experiencing. Dan ran back up the trail toward us.

"I'll help you to the rim, Oma." He took her arm, but she jerked it back.

"No, Danny! It's too dangerous. We must all leave at once!"

"Don't be silly. It's not dangerous. There's just a little storm coming, but we can beat it if you two will just come on."

He glanced at me impatiently then tried to pull Oma's arm again. She stood firm, one hand gripping her cane, the other hand still clenching the black stone.

"Leave her alone, Dan!" I said. "Go get Mom and Dad. This is serious!"

"What's wrong with you?" he shouted back.

"Oma's prediction. I think it's coming true!"

Dan's blue-grey eyes pierced into mine. "You're as crazy as grandma, Ysolde. You're ruining the ceremony. We'll do it without you."

He turned away and headed back toward the rim with the sound of thunder rumbling behind his words.

"No!" Oma shouted as loud as she could. Her eyes flashed at me with a strict look to stay then she headed down the trail.

"Wait!" I watched as she tottered feebly along the steep path. Chill bumps ran up my arm. I felt the warping again. "Kraegon is here!" I yelled. "I feel him!"

Oma looked back at me then stumbled and fell.

"I'm coming!" I ran toward her then something knocked me to the ground. I lay in the dirt, dazed and weak. I couldn't get up. Something invisible was holding me down.

Then, suddenly my chills were replaced with warmth. I heard an unfamiliar male voice. "Ysolde, you will be safe."

I looked up and saw a brilliant shining humanoid figure hovering in the air then a sudden flash of white light blinded me. The force of the light threw me back up the trail away from the rim, away from my family.

The ground began to shake with a loud rumbling like an avalanche. Things began to break loose as the earth shifted beneath me. The forest began collapsing all around. Huge pine trees crashed down. I tried to get up, but my body began sliding toward the mouth of the canyon.

"Dad! Help!" I screamed.

Above the horrid sounds of destruction, above the thunder and howling winds, crashing trees and boulders, I heard my mother screaming in the distance.

"Mom! Where are you?" I shouted.

I rolled onto my stomach and tried to dig my fingers into the dirt, but I was sliding too fast. My mouth and nose filled with debris. Faster and faster I fell. I had to be nearing the edge.

Then the earthquake suddenly stopped and the earth became still. The rocks and trees were silent. My body was no longer sliding. I lay face down, frozen with fear. My ears strained to hear my mother, my father, Dan, Oma. Was there anyone left alive?

My lungs were choked with dust. I coughed and squinted trying to see, but my eyes were caked with dirt. They burned and wept. I rubbed them on my sleeve. My vision slowly began to come back with blurry and mottled images.

I could barely hear what sounded like slow, heavy footsteps behind me in the distance. The steps became louder. Their pace quickened. I looked over my shoulder, straining to see what was coming. A dark form approached rapidly. Kraegon!

I tried desperately to get up and run away. My boots kept sliding out from under me on the loose rocks. Kraegon's shadow was now on top of me.

"No! Get away!" I screamed in terror, holding my hands out in front for defense.

Kraegon leaned toward my face. I thrashed my feet and fists in his direction. My vocal chords seized with fear. He grabbed my arm and pulled me toward him. I swung wildly, trying to hit him.

"Stop!" he yelled. He crushed my body to his chest with bear-like force.

"It's okay. Stop hitting me!" The voice was becoming familiar. "Ysolde – can't you see? It's Dan!"

In the blur, I could barely make out his form. I buried my face in his torn t-shirt. He hugged me, frantically stroking my tangled hair.

"I can't believe you're okay," he said. His voice was shaking and out of breath.

"Where's Mom? Where's Dad?"

Dan didn't answer. I tried to pull away, but his grasp locked me in place.

"What are you doing?" I yelled, pushing my fists against him.

"Stop it!" Dan pressed me so close I could barely breathe.

"Where's Oma? I have to go to the rim!" My body began to tremble with agony. "Please . . ."

Dan was silent. His face was filled with pain. His eyes were swollen with tears.

"There is no rim, Ysolde – the rim is gone."

2. Purgatory

It had been two months since the rim collapsed, taking my parents with it. Presumed dead was not dead in my book. My parents' funerals here in Texas had displayed only photos, no caskets or urns. I was in some sort of purgatory, trapped between the popular assumption that they were dead and my belief that they were somehow still alive and needing me.

Half-empty suitcases and boxes were strewn about my room. I was supposed to be packed and ready to leave for college in the morning. Night had fallen. I lay on my bed, weaving my fingers between the intricate patterns of the coverlet crocheted by Mom and Oma. My paintings of horses and dragons hung on the wall, paintings I had created in a small studio Dad made for me in his workshop when I was twelve. I wouldn't have gotten an art scholarship if it hadn't been for his encouragement. A simple wooden horse he'd carved when I was six stood on the bed stand. I picked it up and stroked the smooth yellow pine. Memories surrounded me. Memories I couldn't wait to leave a few months ago.

The wooden stairs outside my room creaked with a slow, heavy rhythm of someone coming up. The footsteps sounded like Dad; same pace, same weight. I leaped off the bed and jumped toward the door flinging it open just as the steps reached the top landing.

"Whoa! Where are you going in such a rush?" Dan asked.

"Nowhere."

I sat back on my bed, clutching the wooden horse.

"You okay?"

"Why should I be?"

"Because, you're leaving for college in the morning. You haven't even finished packing."

Dan nudged one of my empty boxes with his foot.

"Why does the college have to be so close to *that* place?" The canyon; the place I used to love, the place I now hated.

"Mom and Dad would still want you to go."

"They're not here so none of that matters."

"Stop acting like a spoiled brat. You think it's easy for me? Quitting my job and moving back home to take care of you and Oma wasn't exactly part of my plan."

"I keep thinking Mom and Dad are going to walk through the front door and everything will be okay."

"They're gone, Ysolde."

"No bodies were found."

"They're buried in the rubble at the bottom of the canyon."

"How can you say that so calmly? Don't you care at all?"

"You know I do. But there's nothing we can do. I'm here to take care of things and I can't let my feelings get in the way."

"And now you have to live here and take care of Oma, who may be crazy."

"She's not so bad. She wants to see you in the Burrow." The Burrow was our nickname for Oma's underground house.

"What does she want to see me about?"

"How do I know? Probably some last minute advice or maybe to get you out of this room you've barely left in two months. You're not the only one who's hurting, you know. She blames herself for what happened."

"It's not her fault. It's *my* fault. Oma's prediction was right. I was the one who refused to believe what my pendulum was telling me. Mom and Dad would be here now if I had said something the morning of the ritual. I could've prevented us from going to the rim."

"Mom and Dad's deaths were nobody's fault. They could've dowsed to find out if Oma's prediction was accurate, but they didn't."

"Because they thought Oma was crazy."

"Whatever the reason, it was an accident, a freak earthquake. It's a miracle any of us survived. Now stop this damn self-pity and go see her."

Dan turned to leave then hesitated and looked back at me. "You coming or do I need to carry you out there?" The corners of his mouth rose slightly.

"I'm coming, I'm coming." I said, half-heartedly. I gently set the horse down and drug myself off my bed.

When I opened the back screen door and stepped outside, my body was hit with the thick late August night air. There was a full moon, but there would be no celebration like we used to do. The cicadas were singing loudly in a slow rhythm that rose and fell like a giant heartbeat. The stretch of shadowy field to the Burrow looked unusually long.

I followed the moonlit stone path past Mom's roses and Dad's workshop then Oma's garden. Her Burrow was under a huge mound of earth covered with grass and herbs. The rounded windows on the south side were illuminated with candle light. The path led to the heavy wooden front door my father had carved with images of dragons, inlaid with crystals. I knocked with the pewter dragon's head then waited a few minutes. The door creaked open and Oma peeked out.

"Come in, sweet girl," she said quietly.

"Oma, do you need something?"

"I need you. Come sit with me."

We walked across the oak floor of the intimate room that served as her living room and den. The moon's rays beamed through the windows making the crystals along the sills sparkle. Vines and plants crawled along the walls and overflowing bookcases filled with volumes about dowsing, magick, nature and physics. Authentic medieval tapestries hung from the ceiling. A set of hand carved antique chairs with claw feet and faces of strange beasts were arranged loosely around the room.

I could smell something sweet and familiar coming from the wood cook stove. We walked into the kitchen. Oma gestured for me to sit at her small, wooden table where she had taught me my first lessons in dowsing.

"Medlar pie?" I asked, my mouth already watering.

"Your favorite," Oma said as she wiped flour dust off the table with a cotton hand towel.

Medlar trees were considered rare this far south. Oma had a small grove of them. The fruit had to rot before it was ready to be used then Oma would scoop out the smelly, sweet flesh. It was disgusting to look at, but delicious to taste.

"You haven't made that in years."

"I have a big favor to ask so I thought I better bake something special to bribe you with," she smiled as she dished up a sizeable piece, placing it on a hand-painted china plate.

I bent down to smell the warm, cherished aroma before digging in. She sat and watched me eat for a few minutes. I could tell something serious was on her mind.

"Ysolde, my dear, I'm not sure where to begin." Oma stared at the candle on the table for a moment, lost in thought as she stirred her tea. The flame cast flickering shadows across her face. "There's something about me that you don't know and the time has come to tell you." She reached into her pocket and placed the black stone on the table.

"You know my stone?" she asked.

"You never seem to be without it."

"This stone is very special. It has ancient wisdom. Do you see the markings?"

I picked up the shiny round rock. A warm, tingling sensation danced across my palm. I examined it carefully, dragging my index finger lightly across the surface.

"I feel a tingling."

"That's good," she smiled softly.

"And I see two crossed lines."

"Those lines were carved into the stone many years ago by a shaman from a different world."

"A shaman? Is this another tale?" Oma loved to tell wild tales she claimed were true. Normally, I enjoyed listening to her ramble on and on into the night about strange places and weird creatures, but I wasn't in the mood tonight.

"This is not a tale. I need for you to listen. I am not from this world."

"Oma, this pie is to die for, but I'm tired and sad and I have to leave tomorrow. Can't this wait?"

"I know you're hurting, dear. We all are. It is unfortunate that I must lay this burden on you at such a time. You must go to Abysmal College, but with a different purpose. The other world I speak of *does* exist. It is inside this Earth. If something happens to it, the Earth will perish. We have very little time."

She paused for a moment. Her stare was unusually somber, but what she was saying was ridiculous.

"Inside the Earth? Oma honestly." She ignored me and continued.

"Nearly one thousand years ago, negative energy entities known as Vapors took over the world within Earth to mine the crystal forests. They captured humans and took them to an island known as The End Lands. The humans were held in dungeons and fed upon by the Vapors for their energy. Entire villages began to disappear. Then, by some miracle, positive energy entities known as Lumen appeared. They had followed the Vapors, their mortal enemies, from another dimension. The Lumen fought bravely, but the Vapors were too numerous and strong. Something had to be done before all was destroyed."

Oma paused and took a sip of tea. I stared at her, wondering if she sat in her little burrow all day long dreaming up these fantasies just so she could mess with my mind.

"You should write this one down, Oma. It would make a great bedtime story."

"Ysolde, I am not finished. You *must* listen."

"I'm trying, but you have to admit, this is pretty crazy stuff."

She looked at me sternly then carried on with her story.

"A great shaman known as Nathruk was asked to create a weapon to help the Lumen protect the world within, which is much like medieval Earth except for mystical creatures and magick, of course."

"Of course," I said, pretending to be serious as I scooped the last bit of gooey medlar flesh onto my fork.

"Nathruk went to the ancient land of Shi. There, where the flying Drakenz live, he took a stone from the Primal Waters of the Jaden River and imbued it with magical powers, carving the lines you see now. The stone allowed the Lumen to open a vortex where they could enter the forbidden negative energy world of the Vapors to pursue and destroy them. Without the stone, the world within Earth would surely be void of all life forms and I would never have been born."

"You're talking about *this* little, black stone?"

I humored Oma and examined it more closely. It looked like a plain rock with an X carved into it, nothing more.

"Yes."

"But, if this stone really is so powerful, why do *you* have it?"

"That is an excellent question, my dear. When Nathruk created the stone, he named it Athas and gave it to Gutar, the protector of the Lumen. But, there was one problem. The stone could only be held by the Lumen when they were in human form. As soon as the Lumen changed into their energy form, the stone would drop to the ground. Once on the ground, the stone could be picked up by any human working with the Vapors. This would give the Vapors the power to enter the positive energy fields of the Lumen and destroy them."

Oma took another sip of tea. I kept my mouth shut, trying to be patient.

"To protect the stone," she continued, "Nathruk attached its spirit to a human who was sensitive to positive and negative energies. He chose a dowser from the crystal forest lands of Kalisfaar, my homeland. Her name was Kespara. The Lumen gave her the title of Domina Lumen. I am a direct descendant of her, as are you."

"You mean *you* have the power that Kespara had?"

"Yes."

"That's impressive, Oma."

I stood up and put my plate in the sink. "It's been interesting to hear about this world inside of Earth. You have quite the imagination." I smiled kindly, knowing my grandmother was one step away from the loony bin. I hugged her and started walking toward the door.

"Thanks for the delicious pie. I'll see you in the morning."

Oma struggled to get up then she pounded her cane on the floor with such force I thought it would break.

"Ysolde Nightingale Hartmaan, *sit down*! I am not finished!"

"But, I need to pack for tomorr . . ."

"Tomorrow? There may be no tomorrow!" Oma shook her cane at me and glared with a look I dared not disobey. I sat back down. "You have more reasons than college to return to Abysmal Canyon. You must defeat Kraegon!"

"What?" The atmosphere suddenly felt heavy and suffocating.

"Do you remember Kraegon at the canyon?" She began rubbing the stone vigorously in her palm. She was beyond upset.

"I don't know. I never saw him. Something knocked me to the ground then the world collapsed."

"But you felt his presence," she persisted.

"I felt cold and nauseous. I was caught up in your craziness, that's all."

I looked away, trying not to acknowledge that I actually did see a dark form of some kind in the woods that knocked me to the ground right before the rim collapsed.

"Do you think the deaths of your parents were just *an accident?*" she thundered.

"There was an earthquake. I don't know what happened. Please stop." Tears began to swell in my eyes.

"That was Kraegon trying to kill me for the stone!" Oma's voice was determined. "If it weren't for the Lumen rescuing me, I would be dead and Kraegon would have the stone now. He is a powerful Vapor and has somehow come to Earth. This means the Lumen have lost control of the world within. Kraegon must be stopped before he brings his hordes to this planet. With the help of the Lumen, you are the only one who can stop him!"

"Me? What do I have to do with this?"

I didn't want to listen to this nonsense anymore. I started to leave. Oma grabbed my arm. Her nails pierced my skin.

"Ouch! You're hurting me!"

I tried to pull away. She relaxed her grip, but didn't let go. I felt almost afraid of her.

"Listen to me, Ysolde. I am old and I am frail. I cannot fight him. You are strong and brave. It is time I pass the stone to you. With the help of the Lumen, you will banish Kraegon. You will save the Earth and the world within from the Vapors. You will take vengeance for your parents. *You will be the Domina Lumen!*"

3. First Sight

Night had never looked so black to me. I felt completely alone for the first time in my life, charging up the Colorado mountain pass in my Jeep. Tall pine trees on either side of the highway created a guide through the steep switchbacks. Unseen dangers could leap directly into my path at any time. I had to be vigilant and keep my eyes wide open.

Oma's last words haunted me. "The stone is a burden you must bear, Ysolde. You must go back to Abysmal Canyon and rid the world of this evil."

Use a stone to rid the world of evil? *Evil?* I glanced at the humble black rock lying on the dashboard. It was still hard to take Oma's bizarre story seriously. The reality of it all was too terrifying to be real, even though something did force me to the ground at the canyon and something else prevented me from falling off the rim to my death.

I could see Oma sitting across from me in her kitchen, her face full of moving shadows from the flickering candlelight, the sweet smell of medlar pie lingering in the air.

"You must not let Dan know about the stone," she said. "Such secret knowledge might endanger his life. A Lumen will meet you soon. He is one of the Guardians of the Stone. He has been my protector all these years and now he will protect you. He saved me, you and Dan at the canyon. Unfortunately, he could not save us all.

"Keep Athas safe. Never let the stone out of your sight. It holds great powers that can only be accessed through your skills in dowsing."

I dowsed reluctantly this morning before leaving Texas, afraid of the outcome. I asked two questions. The first, would I have a safe trip to Abysmal College? The pendulum said, "maybe." The second, did Kraegon really exist? The crystal said, "yes." As literal as the pendulum is, a "yes" could mean Kraegon exists in Oma's mind only. I couldn't make myself ask more specifically.

Abysmal College was on the other side of the forest, less than an hour away. The highway had been my sole companion since dawn. It was now almost midnight. I tried not to think of all the times I'd been on this road with my family heading to the canyon for our annual ceremony.

This morning Dan said, "Behave yourself, keep your eyes on the road and watch out for things unknown." He had no idea how relevant those words were.

It was going to be lonely not having him around. At least I would have Cam, Dan's best friend. We were friends in school. He was a junior archaeology student at Abysmal now and the one who encouraged me to apply there. We went on a few dates the summer before he left for college. It was nothing serious, but I really liked him and couldn't wait to see him again.

My eyelids were heavy. My back was stiff. My right ankle ached from pushing the gas pedal. I had never driven so far in one day. I turned my music up and rolled the window down. Cold, pine-scented air rushed inside as I took a sip of stale coffee from the gas station where I had stopped an hour ago. The forest was black and silent. I stared into the shadowy trees hoping to see something that might inject adrenaline into my veins.

A flash of light suddenly caught my eye. It was streaking through the pines then disappeared. I blinked a few times trying to focus then searched for another glimpse. There it was again! The light was moving forward in the woods. It was travelling at an incredible speed and there were more than one.

I sat up straight and strained toward the windshield to see. The three lights swiftly dodged their way through the forest, weaving in and out of the trees. They were growing in intensity as they moved toward the road. I eased my foot off the accelerator. The lights continued to race closer and closer then –

"Shit!" I grabbed the wheel with both hands and slammed on the brakes. Three creatures leaped onto the road directly in front of me. The Jeep skidded sideways. My coffee fell to the floor. The stone flew across the dash board as the car came to an abrupt stop, perched in the middle of the road.

I couldn't move. Fear had taken over my body. One of the creatures had stopped in front of the car and he was staring directly at me. All I could make out was a tall glowing, male humanoid form with long white blonde hair. Windswept strands obscured most of his face. I couldn't take my eyes off him. He turned his head to look at the woods where the others had gone then looked back at me. A strong wave of warm energy surged through my body. I started to sweat then he vanished.

What in the hell was *that*? He looked similar to the glowing humanoid I saw at the canyon right before the rim collapsed. The other two creatures running with him were a smaller humanoid form and what looked like an enormous white wolf.

I looked away from the forest and back at the road. Blinding headlights glared in my windshield. I was directly in the path of a semi-truck barreling down the road toward me at full speed. I floored the Jeep toward the shoulder, wheels squealing. The semi flew past, honking and swerving, barely missing my Jeep by a few yards.

My heart was beating so hard I thought it was going to burst through my chest. Glancing back in the direction of the creatures, I saw nothing but black closing in all around again. *You'll be out of the forest soon. Just hang in there*, I told myself. My hands were shaking as I fumbled to get the top off my water bottle. I took a long, hard drink then grabbed the stone from the dashboard and shoved it into my pocket. Maybe Oma was right. I scanned the area one last time, rolled my window up and eased back onto the highway.

I clung to the steering wheel the last hour on the road, constantly looking over my shoulder and in the rear view mirror. The pendulum said I *might* make it safely, with no guarantees.

I finally reached the small mountain town of Abysmal. It was just after midnight. There were only three motels on the main drag. I chose the closest one. I had to ring the bell to wake the night clerk. He emerged from a back room, looking at me suspiciously. I'm sure I looked like hell. The motel was the older kind where you park your car in front of the door to your room. I lifted the Jeep's tail gate and snatched my backpack then hurried inside, locking the door behind me.

This was the first time I had stayed at a motel alone. The small room reeked of cigarettes. Creepy shadows were in every corner even with all the lights on; not exactly comforting considering the recent scare of my life. I was tempted to call Dan, but didn't.

I jammed a chair under the handle of the door as Dan had instructed me to do. It made me feel a little better although I knew the act was strictly symbolic. It might deter a human, but nothing like a flimsy chair shoved against a door would stop an entity like Kraegon or those glowing humanoid creatures.

Oma had told me to unplug all electrical devices in the room because the entities could travel through electricity. Her advice didn't sound so weird now. I pulled the plugs on the T.V., radio alarm clock and coffee maker. I brushed my teeth, washed my face then kicked off my tennis shoes, keeping my clothes on just in case I needed to run outside. Athas was still secure in my pocket. My crystal pendant was safely around my neck. I unplugged the lamp and jumped into bed, determined not to close my eyes, but nature eventually took over.

~ Dream ~

He was standing on the rim of a canyon next to the edge of a yawning chasm. It was night. The moon was a waning sliver in the sky. He wore jeans, a black tee shirt and hiking boots. I felt his cold energy drawing me near. I walked toward him in the haze. Grey eyes calmly stared into mine as he waited for my approach.

His pale face was strong and beautiful; his body lean and powerful. Wind rising vertically up from the base of the canyon blew his long black hair in a swirl around his neck. Everything was in slow motion. I couldn't feel my boots touching the ground as I walked uphill, entranced.

I stood before him. His lips curved upwards as his eyes locked onto mine. His pale hand touched my face, caressing my cheek then stroking my bottom lip with his thumb. The skin on his hand felt cold and soft. It was almost transparent in color with tiny flecks of light surging just beneath the surface. He leaned down, his mouth inches from my face. He lingered for a few moments then his lips gently enveloped mine. They were cool and soft. I closed my eyes, feeling cold sparks rush through my body. I couldn't move. I didn't want to move.

The rush was exhilarating. My heart beat wildly without rhythm. He inhaled my breath, forcefully rubbing his slick lips against mine. He laughed softly into my breath then pulled away, his eyes continuing to observe mine.

He turned his head and gracefully walked away toward the gorge. At the edge, he leapt off the rim into the abyss. I gasped in horror. But he didn't fall. He stood in midair, on an invisible bridge of some sort. He turned back toward me. His eyes were no longer black, but glowing white. He reached out in my direction, his long, pale fingers radiating electrical energy.

I took a few steps forward, staring down at the gaping, black void before me. My toes hung over the edge. The pit of my stomach lodged in my throat. Small rocks under my boots began breaking loose. I watched as they plunged silently into the emptiness below. The man's strong energy inched my body forward. My boots barely clung to the precipice now. I looked into his pale beautiful face nodding at me with confidence and encouragement. I trusted him. I loved him. I would die for him. I took his hand and stepped off the rim.

4. First Love

I woke with a start from my dream just in time before hitting the jagged rocks at the bottom of the canyon. I breathed a sigh of relief to be alive. Grey light of early dawn was leaking from the edge of the motel room curtains. It was too early to call Dan, but I called him anyway.

"Mmmm, hello?" Dan answered after the fourth ring. His voice was groggy and rough.

"Hey, bro!"

"Who's this?" He said with a sleepy chuckle.

"You're funny. I'm in Abysmal! It took me thirteen hours." I prepared to tell him all about my big adventure.

"That's great," he yawned. "Glad you're alive. Call me back after you've moved into the dorm." Click.

"Wait! Dammit."

Dan wasn't a morning person. I was bursting to tell someone about my trip, the close encounter on the mountain and the mysterious man in my dream. Oma wouldn't talk on a phone because of the electromagnetic energy. I didn't have any close friends I could tell. Dan was the only one.

Cam was supposed to help me move into the dorm this morning. I told him I'd call around 9:00. I had two hours to kill. I got out of bed and glanced out the window through the stiff rubberized curtains. The glass felt cold to the touch. My faithful Jeep was still parked right outside the door.

I moved the chair from the doorknob, unlocked the deadbolt and chain then rushed out in my wrinkled clothes to grab my suitcase from the car. The chilly mountain air was energizing. I scanned the immediate area for shadowy forms then ran back inside.

After a quick shower, I dressed, making sure to take the stone out of my old jeans and put it in the pocket of my clean jeans. My stomach growled. It'd been twenty-four hours since I'd eaten anything substantial. I slipped my jacket on and walked to the lobby to grab the free continental breakfast that came with the room.

There were a few fellow early risers in the eating area sitting around small tables arranged in a crowded cluster. Most of them looked like outdoor types. A flat screen T.V. mounted on the wall showed the local morning news. A student who'd been camping near the rim of the canyon was apparently now missing. Her tent and gear had been found, but she was nowhere in the area. My stomach lurched. Could Kraegon have had anything to do with her disappearance?

I poured coffee into a foam cup, added lots of milk and took a few bagels and oranges back to the room. Nine o'clock finally came and I called Cam.

"Ysolde! You're here!"

His bright, cheerful voice sounded good. We talked briefly, catching up in a few short sentences. I wanted to tell him about my scary night, but wasn't sure I should. We agreed to meet in the parking lot nearest my dorm. I paid for my room then jumped into the Jeep, my heart pounding with happiness and inescapable fear.

The dorm parking lot was already full of parents and students unloading their possessions when I arrived. My eyes scanned the horizon, looking at the surrounding mountains. Just a few months ago I saw beauty and nature in them. Now I saw danger and death.

"Hey girl!" Cam's unmistakable strong, warm voice came from behind. I turned and saw his hunky frame walking in my direction. He was grinning from ear to ear.

Cam had matured in all the right ways. He still had his striking white smile with a cute dimple in one cheek and soft green eyes. The shadow on his face from not shaving looked sexy and natural. His brunette hair was down to his shoulders. Lean muscles were obvious through his tight white tee shirt. He was wearing old jeans with holes in the knees and hiking sandals, practically barefoot. The chilly air didn't seem to faze him.

"Hey!" I beamed, looking at his eager face. He took two long strides and gave me a big hug almost as tight as Dan's vise grip. His energy was kind and inviting. I briefly snuggled my face into his soft cotton shirt. He smelled like pine needles and freshly cut wood.

"You're looking good." He stepped back to take a long gaze at me.

"Thanks, you too." I looked down at the asphalt for a few seconds, wishing I'd worn something a little sexier than an oversized sweater. He cocked his head sideways, his eyes trying to catch mine. I looked back at him and smiled.

"So, you're really going to help me with this?" I stammered, trying to get past the awkward moment.

"Of course, doesn't look like you brought much, though." He gazed into the back of the Jeep.

"I don't need a lot. I'm a *non*-material girl," I smirked.

"Yeah, I remember. I always liked that about you." His eyes softened. "Listen, I'm sorry about your mom and dad."

"Thanks." I hoped he wouldn't ask any details about their deaths.

"I'm sorry I couldn't make it to the funeral. What happened?" Well crap. I didn't blame him for asking. He knew my folks and they liked him. I could feel the sadness welling up inside and I didn't want it to. I wanted to be happy.

"I'd rather not talk about it." I could feel my eyes burning and getting moist.

"I'm sorry. I shouldn't have . . ."

"It's okay. Don't worry about it."

Cam gently wrapped his arms around me, rubbing my back. I fought back the urge to let loose a flood of emotions. Cam represented home. He was like family. After a few minutes he pulled away.

"Are you alright?"

"Yeah. I'll be fine." I blinked back the tears.

"You should probably go in the dorm and find your room before we start unloading."

"Right." I forced myself to get my act together.

"I'll start getting things out while you go do that."

"Okay, I'll be back in a sec."

It was a relief having someone take Dan's place so soon. I didn't mind letting Cam give me orders – anything to help me get through this.

When I reached the front door of the dorm, a bubbly sorority girl with a red tee shirt and long auburn ponytail greeted me. She found my name on her clip board then cheerfully led me down the hall as if this was the most important job in the world. How could anyone be so happy?

My room was on the second floor, directly across from the communal bathroom, the other thing I was dreading apart from having a roommate. My roomy wasn't there when I entered, but her cotton candy essence was. Everything was pink. The ruffles on the bedspread, a ceramic heart that read "I heart Tiff," the lacey curtains, the oval shag rug, the silk scarf draped over the desk lamp – all shades of bubblegum and rose.

Numerous stuffed animals adorned her bed. Some were old with missing eyes and limbs, many with bows around their necks. I didn't know girls like this existed beyond eighth grade.

I felt my first pangs of homesickness. My room at home looked like a natural science museum with rocks, crystals, bones, leaves, shells and other objects I'd found in the fields on my walks. All types of plants adorned the window sills. My bedspread was a green and blue batik design of organic shapes. Lying under the covers in my room at home felt like being in an ancient, mystical forest.

I groaned quietly, sitting down on the naked single mattress of my lonely little bed on the gloomy side of the room. It was time to get Cam so he could talk me out of jumping into my Jeep and heading back home.

I walked back to the parking lot. Cam was waiting patiently, sitting on the bumper of the Jeep playing a game on his phone.

"Ready?" he said.

"Yeah, I guess," I sighed.

"What's wrong?"

"Oh, you'll see," I managed a tight grin, trying not to come across as the spoiled brat Dan said I had become.

We both grabbed an arm load and headed to my room.

"Oh, wow," he chuckled when he saw the pink palace. "This is definitely *not* you."

"Ya think?"

"Well, you'll be okay. You're flexible." He set the box down on my bed.

"Are you kidding me?" I stared at him, waiting for a more sympathetic response.

"Oh, come on. It's not going to be *that* bad. You probably won't be spending that much time in your room anyway. As I recall, you like to spend all your time in the studio doing your art, right?"

"Well, yeah."

"So, no big deal. Come on, let's get the rest of your stuff."

How little he knew. I didn't come to college to do my art. This was all a ruse. My real purpose for being here was to destroy some supernatural evil energy entity and save the world with a rock – like that's going to happen.

I followed him back to the Jeep. We spent the next hour bringing my things up to the room and talking. I decided to leave my camping gear in the car just in case I needed a night away from the pink queen.

On our last load, a girl in a room down the hall introduced herself as Alia Murphy. She was petite like me with shoulder length brunette hair and chocolate eyes. She dressed simply in skinny jeans and a green tee shirt with snowy mountains printed on the front. She was a sophomore and also an art major. Cam seemed especially attracted to her.

"You're welcome to come to my room anytime, Ysolde. I know it's a little awkward being a freshman. I'll be glad to introduce you to some of my friends." Her eyes twinkled at Cam.

"Thanks," I said.

"See ya later." She turned and headed down the hall toward the stairs.

"She seems nice," said Cam, watching her walk away.

I punched him gently in the arm. He turned and looked at me.

"What? Don't I get to look?" He grinned.

I started to say something then realized I'd sound like a jealous girlfriend. I had to remember that Cam and I were just old friends, nothing more.

"Never mind," I said.

"I was just being polite and she does have nice jeans."

"Okay," I chuckled, trying to keep it light.

I had to be careful not to spoil things between us. Cam was my lifeline, my surrogate brother for this year and I needed his friendship. I needed someone who understood me, who knew my family, who would accept me for who I was, no matter what.

We walked down to the Jeep. I grabbed the last box.

"Think you can handle it from here?" he said.

"Please, don't go. I was just kidding about Alia."

"I know. It's not that. I have things I need to do. I'll call you later to see how things are going, okay?"

"Okay. Thanks for all your help."

I watched Cam walk across the parking lot. My heart fractured a little, like it did yesterday when Dan disappeared in my rear view mirror as I drove away from home. I breathed a heavy sigh.

I'm not sure I can do this. My parents are presumed dead. Dan's not here. I can't talk to Oma on the phone. I have no idea when I'll meet the mysterious Lumen man. I'm supposed to rid the world of some evil entity named Kraegon with just a stone while using my dowsing skills, which are minimal at best. I'm living away from home for the first time and I'm starting college with an adolescent roommate who's obsessed with the color pink. Could it get any worse?

5. Pink Queen

I started unpacking my boxes. Most were crammed with clothes and art supplies, but a few held my treasures, my favorite rocks, candles, books and photos.

A high pitched chipmunk voice suddenly chirped from behind.

"Hey! You must be Ysolde!" I knew without looking that this must be my much anticipated pink partner for the year.

She waltzed through the doorway and plunked down on her bed grabbing a pink stuffed pig. She was dressed in tight jeans with a blue and gold football jersey tied at her slender waist. On her feet were pink, high-heeled sandals. Tied around her long, blonde ponytail was a pink bow. She wore gaudy gold hoop earrings and bright pink lip gloss on her full lips. I felt certain she was eye candy to every jock on campus.

"Tiff?" I said, forcing myself to smile.

"In the flesh! Where's all your stuff?" She glanced around at my meager belongings.

"You're looking at it. I didn't have room to bring a lot in the car."

"Oh, right. You're from out of town."

Tiff kissed the pig on the nose. "Don't worry. I'll help you fit in. Say, do you have a boyfriend?"

"What?"

"Boyfriend – do you have one?"

"Kind of." My pride would not let me admit that I was single. I refused to start off at the dorm with a loser reputation.

"Well, if you're lookin', I know a guy who would be perfect for you. He's a jock and he's gorgeous. He just had a nasty breakup with a skank I'll tell you about later. His name is Derek. Do you like chocolate ice cream? I *love* chocolate ice cream. I have some in the mini fridge if you want any. And, where are you from again?" Tiff stopped to take a breath.

"Texas."

"Oh, *Texas*," she snickered. "You know what they say about girls from Texas, don't you?"

"Please, enlighten me."

Seriously? How was I going to live with this person all year long? Maybe I could set my tent up on campus somewhere or live in my Jeep.

"Girls from Texas have big boobs and little brains," she snorted, kissing the little pig again.

I decided to be nice and play along. I looked down at my nearly flat chest and said with a grin, "Obviously, they haven't met me." We both laughed. "I guess since we're both blondes, we won't be telling any blonde jokes, right?" I hoped.

Tiff's eyes lit up. "I get bombarded with blonde jokes all the time, but they don't bother me since I'm not really a blonde."

"Ahh," was all I could politely respond with.

Two girls showed up at the door with armloads of chips, dip and drinks. They looked like they came from the same candy mold as Tiff.

"Tiffy, where do you want this party stuff?" One of them asked between blowing and smacking bubbles with her gum.

Tiff gestured toward her desk. "Looks good, ladies. Did you get the-you-know-what?" she raised one eyebrow. The one with the gum reached into a bag and pulled out two six packs of wine coolers.

"Now that's what I'm talkin' bout," Tiff giggled. "These are just for us girls," she winked as she put them in the packed little dorm frig.

"I'm Val and this is Mandy," said the gum chewer. They began taking chips and dip and other snacks out of the bags. "And you are?"

"I'm Ysolde. Are we having a party, Tiff?" As if it wasn't obvious.

"Tiff's room is party central in this dorm. Everyone knows that!" Val giggled, flipping her black ponytail.

"We're having a welcome back blowout tonight," Tiff said.

"Sounds fun." I faked my enthusiasm, trying to accept the reality that my room was apparently a jock groupie flop house.

What was wrong with me? I should be excited that my roomy was the queen of all parties. It wasn't the idea of a party that bothered me. It was the idea of the party being in my room. I wouldn't have a refuge to go to. I needed my rest. I was supposed to be saving the world, for Pete's sake.

"Okay, see you girls tonight. I can't wait!" Mandy said as the two girls raced out of the room.

"Can I help with anything?" I asked out of sheer politeness, thinking of my mom who had raised me to always offer help, no matter what. This was going to be a true test.

"Thanks, but the girls and I will do all the work. You just stick around and have fun! Oh, hey – did you hear about that girl they found in the canyon? She was found lying next to the river with a broken neck. It's sooo gross."

Tiff lay back on her bed, picking up a blue elephant with one eye and a torn ear.

"Was that the missing girl who'd been camping?"

"Yeah, I think so. They said it looked like suicide. She was in one of my classes last year. She seemed happy enough. It's just weird."

She stared out the window next to her bed and became quiet for the first time since we'd met. She seemed to actually be having a serious thought.

"Hey babe!" A loud booming voice suddenly came from out in the hall. We both jumped, startled at the break in silence.

"Tanner!" squealed Tiff, flinging the little elephant across the room, running toward the door. "Oh my God, you look *amazing!*" I turned and looked at the huge hunk of guy blocking the doorway. "You worked out this summer, didn't you?" she cooed, hugging him and caressing his massive chest and biceps.

"Yea, babe. Who's this?"

"That's Ysolde, my new roomy," she said in a sexy voice while she drew a heart on his chest with her finger.

"Hey," Tanner nodded at me with a big grin, his eyes wandering around my body as if he could see right through my sweater.

Tiff stood on her tip toes and pulled his face back toward her. She gave Tanner a neglected puppy dog look with pouty lips. He picked her up effortlessly then kissed her passionately as he carried her to the bed.

I watched the two of them embrace as stuffed animals were hurled onto the floor. They obviously knew each other quite well. The fact that I was in the room wasn't slowing their agenda down one bit.

"Um, I think I'll just check out the campus for a bit. See you guys tonight." I turned to leave. Tiff waved briefly in my direction. Tanner winked at me and smirked. I got the feeling he'd be perfectly fine if I wanted to stay and join in the fun. No doubt this was going to be a common event in our room. I closed the door to the pink love nest and sighed.

Abysmal College was different than most campuses. The men and women who founded the school had been naturalists and planned the layout around the existing trees and natural landforms. The dirt paths connecting the buildings were shaded by groves of elder pine, spruce, cottonwood and aspen. The back side of the campus ran next to a wilderness area.

I hiked around, checking out the main points of interest and saved the best for last. The art building was at the edge of campus with the forest right behind it. The two-story adobe building with one side made of glass gave it a greenhouse effect. My first painting class would be there Monday morning.

Time had gotten away from me. The sun had dropped behind the mountains. The chilly night air was setting in. I headed to the bookstore cafe to grab a quick bite before going back to the dorm. As I was picking up my order of grilled cheese and small fries, Alia walked by with a sack full of books.

"Hey, Alia. Looks like you've got a load," I grinned.

"I just spent my entire life's savings," she laughed.

"Want to join me?" I walked over to a table by the window.

"Sure." She pulled up a chair.

I had a sudden painful flashback of eating supper at home with Mom and Dad. Supper was a time when we would share thoughts about our day. I looked out the window and forced myself not to get emotional.

"You okay?" Alia asked.

"Do you like to hike?" I dodged her question.

"Love it. I also love skiing, rock climbing and kayaking. How about you?"

"Hiking and skiing, although my skiing is more like rolling downhill, in which I excel."

"Just takes practice. I was the same way when I started. I couldn't even get off the ski lift without falling flat on my face in front of everybody. They'd have to stop the lift and help me up. So embarrassing!"

"Been there."

"I'm going hiking next Saturday with some of my friends. Why don't you come along? You could bring your cute boyfriend, Cam."

"Oh, he's not my boyfriend." Why in the hell did I just tell her that, even if it was the truth?

"Oh really?"

"I mean, we're good friends. We're *very* close. Anyway, I think he has an archaeology dig that weekend. He goes to those all the time." A little white lie never hurt anyone.

"That's too bad."

"But I might be interested. Where are you guys going?"

"We'd probably go to the canyon, along the rim maybe."

"The rim? Isn't that where that girl was found dead?"

"Actually, her tent was on the rim. She was found at the bottom by the river. It's a big canyon, Ysolde. But if that makes you nervous, we could hike in the woods near the canyon."

"I think I'll pass. Thanks anyway."

"Come on. You're not *afraid* are you?" Alia pressed, raising an eyebrow.

What was that all about? She had been super friendly until now. I wasn't sure I liked her sudden, aggressive tone. I didn't like being accused of being afraid, whether it was true or not, especially not by someone I just met. She had no idea what was out there.

"It's not that."

"Look, we'll have two big guys and another girl with us. No one is going to attack a group of five. You'll be safe."

"Isn't there some place else to hike around here?"

"Sure, there are lots of places. I'll tell you what – you agree to go and I promise we'll stay clear of the canyon and the woods in that area. How does that sound?

"So – no canyon."

"I promise. No canyon."

"Okay, sounds good." I had damn good reasons for staying away from that canyon. I didn't feel comfortable telling Alia about my parent's deaths. And of course, there was Kraegon.

"Great! We'll be leaving around 10:00 next Saturday. Just come to my room."

"Are you going to Tiff's party tonight?"

Alia laughed, "No way! I'm steering clear of our entire floor. Tiff and Tanner's parties are legendary. I'm staying at my friend's house, off campus. Guess you have to go since it's in your room, huh?"

"Yep, lucky me. Speaking of, I guess I should start heading in that direction."

"Have fun," she kidded.

"You know it. I'll see you later."

We parted company and I reluctantly started my trek over to the party palace.

As I approached the dorm, I could see a rosy glow coming from our window on the second story. It was lit with tiny multi-colored blinking lights and a sign facing out to the world that read "Party Here!" Great.

When I entered the building, the first floor was fairly tame with a few quiet "welcome back" parties going on. Not so bad.

I walked up the stairs to the second floor. The hall was packed with students. A loud thumping beat reverberated against the walls. I squeezed my way through the crowd. Several rooms had their doors open and students were milling in and out. The music was coming from my room, or should I say Tiff's room. No surprise there.

My doorway was blocked by three giant hulks wearing blue and gold tee shirts with the face of a roaring bear, the college mascot, printed on the front. Some of Tanner's friends, I assumed. I wedged between their massive bodies.

They raised their drinks above my head, grinning down at me.

The room was dimly lit with hundreds of tiny multi-colored blinking lights strung around the walls and draped across the ceiling in a zigzag pattern. They created an atmosphere I actually liked of beautiful twinkling stars.

Tiff and Tanner were sitting on her bed, surrounded by her loyal stuffed animals. Tiff had put little party hats on each one – the queen and king on their throne surrounded by their subjects. Mandy and Val were dancing with one of the hulks. Two girls were dancing barefoot with each other on the pink shag rug. A tall guy was standing alone in the corner, more interested in watching the couple who was kissing on my bed than eating his plate of chips and dip. Another girl sat at the edge of my bed, awkwardly alone and very much aware of the couple right next to her. Someone had covered my bed with a blanket. I was thankful considering what might take place there later tonight without me.

Everyone looked like normal humans – a little wasted, but normal. No one looked like a Lumen who had come to the party to find me or a Vapor who had come to kill me. I had no idea when or where I would meet the man Oma spoke of or *if* I would meet him at all.

"Ysolde!" hooted Tiff, smiling and holding up a wine cooler. Her eyes were bloodshot and beginning to cross. Tanner gave a goofy grin in my direction. I nodded at them both, trying my best to be a good sport. "Hey, grab a drink and come on over! That's Derek!" Tiff slurred, pointing at one of the beefsteaks dancing in the doorway. "Derek! Say hi!" the pink queen commanded, motioning in my direction.

"Hey!" Derek shouted, beaming at me with perfect teeth. I gave a half wave in his direction. He was cute, but not my type. I needed a brain to go with that brawn.

The fridge was empty. The girls had managed to polish off the wine coolers. I helped myself to a cold soda then stood around, feeling awkward. I tried to talk over the music to the girl sitting on my bed, but it was no use. This was clearly a party to hook up with someone. The only topic of conversation was who'd broken up over the summer and who was available.

I envied Alia having friends she could spend the night with. Maybe this would be a good time to call Dan. I grabbed my jacket and exited the room without anyone noticing.

Not far from the dorm was a cluster of old stone benches sitting in a grove of aspen trees. It looked like a quiet place to sit and give Dan a quick call. I punched in his number and he answered in just a few rings.

"Hey! So tell me, how is it?" he asked. I became homesick the minute I heard his voice.

"It's great!" I choked a little on the words. I needed to sound positive no matter how hard it was. I wanted to talk to him so badly about my fear of what was to come with the Lumen, the Vapors and Kraegon, but I couldn't put his life at risk so I kept the conversation about Tiff and Cam and my trip.

"My roommate's having a big party in our room right now."

"Cool! And you're not there because . . ."

"I wanted to call you. How are you?"

"I'm fine. Tell me about your roommate."

"You have such a one tract mind!" I laughed.

"Yeah, I do, so tell me."

"Well, Tiff is apparently a very popular girl."

"Tiff, eh? I'm looking forward to meeting her," Dan chuckled.

"She's just your type, a very pretty, skinny, high maintenance party girl."

"She sounds perfect!"

"With a giant, football player boyfriend she's madly in love with," I added.

"Not so perfect. Oh well, easy come, easy go. Did Cam show up?"

"He helped me move in this morning. He's looking good."

"Tell him thanks for me. So, everything else is going okay?"

"No complaints so far," I lied.

"How was your drive up?"

"It was long. I had a crazy thing happen last night in the forest. I nearly hit something running across the highway."

"You need to watch out for the deer up there. Remember how they used to come out of nowhere when Dad drove us to the canyon?"

"Yeah, thanks for bringing that memory up."

"You're too sensitive."

"Whatever. I'm sure they weren't deer. They were glowing."

"Glowing? Like aliens?" Dan laughed.

"Yes, two humanoids and a wolf."

"Okaaay."

"One stopped to look at me. He was the freakiest thing I've ever seen."

"You sound like Oma. Are you sure you weren't imagining things?"

"It was real. I swear."

"Maybe you should report it as a UFO sighting," he chuckled.

"Never mind. Geez." I knew it sounded crazy. Even I wouldn't believe it if I hadn't seen it.

"So, how is Oma?" I asked.

"Oh, we're having a real ball here," he said sarcastically. "She did make me a medlar pie, though."

"I'm jealous."

"Ha-ha. You should be."

"I need for you to give her a message. Tell her I need to know when and where the man is going to show up."

"The man?"

"She'll know."

"I'll talk to her later and send you a text."

"Can't you talk to her now?"

"She's probably asleep. I need to go. Some of my friends are here at the house. Glad things are going well."

"Text me first thing in the morning with Oma's reply, okay?"

"You worry too much. Go back to the party and make some friends and have some fun. Talk to you later." Click.

Dammit. I know Dan. He's not going to ask Oma anything.

I put my phone in my pocket and looked up at the sky. The night was heavenly. The full moon was beginning to wane, but still cast enough light to create shadows among the trees.

I didn't want to go back to the party. Instead, I started to head toward the library when a sudden tingling then a cold shiver ran through me. A quick wave of dizziness followed. I froze in place. Could it be Kraegon?

A guy suddenly appeared out of nowhere. He walked by, uncomfortably close. His face was concealed by his hoodie. He looked like a student, but it was hard to tell. He glanced at me as he passed, but I couldn't see his face. At that very moment the chills were replaced by warmth and I began to sweat.

Those were the same strange sensations I experienced in the canyon and on the road with the glowing humanoid man. Either I was having some weird hormonal fluctuations or that guy that just passed was the Lumen guy. Why didn't he stop?

I started following him, keeping my distance. He walked to the art building then went behind it to a dirt trail. The path led into the forest. I stopped at the trail head and watched him disappear among the trees. My intuition was screaming for me to go back to the dorm where it was safe, despite the party.

My feet stood motionless as I stared into the woods. The moon infused a light grey aura upon the trees. My eyes squinted, straining to see. My ears were hypersensitive to sounds of danger. Everything was deadly quiet except my thumping heartbeat.

Tall black pines at the trail head stood erect like guardians of a forbidden realm, warning me not to come closer. I inhaled a lungful of cold crisp air. Goosebumps ran up my spine. My muscles quivered involuntarily. Should I go in? I had to find out. I needed to know if this was the Lumen man. I needed answers. *This wouldn't be the first time I'd done something totally stupid. Hopefully it wouldn't be my last.*

6. Second Sight

I took a few steps onto the trail and stopped, reaching into my pocket to make sure Athas was still there. The stone's smooth, worn surface reassured me, even though I had no clue how to use it. I gathered my courage and warily began walking forward.

I hiked for about a quarter of a mile without seeing any more signs of the man. A normal, sane person would turn around at this point and get the hell out while she still could. She wouldn't have even entered the forest in the first place. But for some unknown, ridiculous reason, I couldn't make myself leave. Something in my gut was telling me that if I could force myself to stay in the forest a little while longer, the Lumen man might come to me.

I looked for a place to wait. In the dim light, not too far off the path was a large fallen tree. I cautiously approached the log and sat down. It wasn't long before my skin began to feel warm. I nervously looked around, but didn't see anyone. The back of my neck began to sweat. *Here we go. He must be near.* The heat continued to rise. I unzipped my jacket to let in some cool air. Beads of sweat began to form on my forehead.

Then suddenly I felt a strong, magnetic sensation similar to the feeling I had in my dream with the floating man who pulled me off the canyon rim. I grasped the log to steady my position. My flushed face felt tingly as if it were being pelted with tiny, soft sparks. I became a little disoriented and woozy.

I could feel someone or *something* looking at me. I turned and tried to see down the trail in the dark, but there was nothing obvious. When I turned back, glowing figures were rushing through the trees not too far away. My heart froze. I held my breath.

The forms made no sounds as they raced together in a streaking blur. My eyes widened as I realized I was seeing the same two humanoids and wolf I had nearly hit on the road on my drive to Abysmal.

I ducked down behind the log and watched as they came closer. This was really happening. I was about to find out if they were friendly – or not. I presumed if they were the Lumen, they were friends with Oma. But what did I know about energy entities?

The smaller humanoid and the wolf suddenly dashed back into the dark out of sight, but the larger humanoid remained. He took a few steps forward into a small clearing less than ten yards away from me. I could see he had the same long white hair as the glowing man I saw on the road. The humanoid's radiance quickly dissipated and he instantly morphed into an actual human dressed in jeans and a t-shirt.

Seeing the glowing humanoids again was terrifying enough, but watching one morph into a human right before my eyes was insane. And with clothes? How does that work? Is his form some kind of an illusion?

He started walking toward me. I thought I was going to die from heart failure. I had waited here to speak with him and here he was, in the flesh, so to speak. And now I didn't have the courage to say anything. All I wanted to do was run back to the dorm. I leapt from behind the log like a scared little rabbit flushed from a bush. My jeans snagged on a broken branch. I stumbled backwards then jerked my leg violently, ripping my pants, but yanking myself free.

I ran back down the trail, tripping on rocks and fallen branches. My pace was too frantic and clumsy. I lost the narrow, unmarked path and found myself racing deeper into the forest. Pine boughs slapped me in the face, their sharp needles scraping my cheeks and neck. I thrust my arms out in front of me to provide some form of protection and kept running.

The high elevation soon took over. I could barely breathe. My lungs ached for air. I stopped and leaned down with both hands on my knees for a moment. My body temperature cooled off as the night chill set in. I zipped up my jacket and glanced around, having no idea where the trail was now.

Maybe the man had gone back to the others. How could he be Oma's Lumen man, my so-called *guardian*? Why would he want to scare me half to death like that? Even though he didn't actually do anything harmful, he could have said something to ease my fear. Maybe he couldn't speak English. Maybe he couldn't speak at all. Oma gave me absolutely zero information on how to communicate with him.

I caught my breath and calmed down a bit then started hiking quickly in the direction I thought might be the way out. A wave of heat suddenly came over me. *Here we go again.* He must be near. I turned to go a different direction, but the warming sensation continued. He must be following me. My eyes stung with tears of fear. I could keep hiking blindly through the trees, hoping I might eventually stumble my way out of the woods or I could stop and hide.

There was a tall pine with a wide girth nearby. I dropped to the ground beside the trunk and pulled Athas out of my pocket. It was supposed to have all kinds of power; maybe it could create some kind of force field around me. *I wish.* Even if it could, I wouldn't have a clue as to how to make it work. The heat around me became more intense. I pulled my knees close to my body and tried to become invisible with the tree.

Then something suddenly grabbed my shoulder from behind. Warm firm fingers pressed deep into my skin. I leapt from the tree and dashed wildly into the dark. My body slammed directly into the trunk of another tree. I reeled backwards in pain and fell to the ground into a deep bed of pine needles. The bark cut the skin on my forehead and a warm trickle of blood began running down my face.

As I scrambled to get up, I realized I had dropped Athas. I dove back to the ground, furiously running my hands through the twigs, needles and leaves. My fingernails dug through the dirt, grabbing every rock, blindly feeling for the correct shape and size of the ancient stone.

The mysterious man had to be able to hear me rustling about. I tried to be quiet as my fingers continued scouring the area. Sweat and blood oozed from my forehead. His heat was enveloping me in a fog.

A sinister shadow darkened the moon light around me. I looked up. There he was, standing just a few feet away still in his human form.

"I won't hurt you," he said. His voice was confident and deep. The fact that he actually could speak made him all too real. I froze in terror, crouching on the ground like a frightened cat.

"Do not be afraid. I have something for you." He held out his hand. I stayed on the ground, motionless. "You dropped it. It is of great importance. Please, take it."

I slowly stood up, keeping my body hunched over and tense in self-defense mode. My trembling, dirt-encrusted fingers reached forward. He placed a stone in my hand. A strong surge of energy passed from his fingertips to mine. My heart beat erratically for a moment.

I turned the stone over in my palm. As soon as I felt the familiar lines I knew it was Athas.

"Thank you," was all I could mumble through my quivering lips.

The mysterious man stood silently. My eyes skimmed his broad chest and lean build. He stared into my eyes as if memorizing my soul.

In the moonlight, I could see that his facial features were elegantly rugged. His eyes were light in color. He looked older than me, perhaps in his late twenties or early thirties.

"You're lost. I can help," he finally said. He reached up to touch my bleeding forehead. I jerked back. He smiled softly. "I'm not the one you should be afraid of." He turned his head towards the woods then looked back at me. "There's someone who wishes to harm you. He's been watching you tonight. Let me show you the way out of the forest." His eyes gazed at the crystal pendant around my neck.

This was the time to ask if he was Oma's Lumen.

"Are you. . ?

He interrupted me before I could finish.

"I'll walk ahead. You can follow," he said as he turned away.

The man began hiking briskly through the trees. I had to jog to keep up. I followed at a safe distance; all the while nervously watching behind me for whatever it was he said was in the forest wanting to harm me.

We hadn't gone too far when I saw the familiar trail dimly appear up ahead. I had never been so happy to see a dirt trail in all my life. I followed the man along the path toward the lights of the campus. He stopped at the trail head just behind the art building where I'd begun this hellish nightmare.

I felt a little less frightened of the man since he had led me to safety and I was so close to campus now. I tried to ask him again.

"Are you the Lumen man I'm supposed to meet?"

Without answering, he suddenly morphed back into his glowing form right in front of me then disappeared.

I'll take that as a no. I sprinted as fast as I could back to the dorm.

When I arrived at my room, the party was over and all was quiet. Tiff was sprawled across her bed, still in her party clothes. Her cheeks were covered with red heart stickers someone had gently applied like little love tattoos.

The room was a wreck. Empty soda bottles, pink plastic cups and party plates with leftover food littered the floor and furniture. Bags of leftover burgers and fries were strewn about. A squished hot apple pie lay in the center of the pink rug. The twinkling lights hanging from the ceiling were decorated with two bras, one pink polka dot and one black lace. But none of that mattered to me. I was safe, for the moment.

I fumbled around in the dark until I found my bag of toiletries and my bath towel then shuffled across the hall to the bathroom. The bloody scrape on my forehead from the trees had begun to swell and crust over. The area around the cut had turned into a tender blue-green bruise the size of a small egg. Pine needles and leaves were entangled in my hair. My hands and broken nails were covered with dirt and pine sap. I looked like the female version of the Celtic Green Man except bloody and battle worn. Tomorrow was the first day of class. It would take some major makeup to hide my wounds.

I picked the debris from my hair and took a quick shower then headed back to the room. I placed Athas under my pillow then set my alarm and crawled into my nest. My mattress was stiff and uncomfortable, but I didn't care. I pulled my comforter up to my chin and breathed a sigh of relief. I had survived the second day of being on my own. One hell of a day.

The curtains on the window next to Tiff's bed were open. I stared at the eerie tree shadows dancing across the pane. I knew I couldn't sleep knowing something *might* be staring at me. I jumped up and jerked the curtains closed, then leaped back into my bed.

Even though I was exhausted, it seemed to take eternity for me to relax enough to go to sleep. After many deep breaths and attempts to clear my mind of the terrifying events of the day, I finally began to doze off.

A vision of the mysterious man from the forest began to emerge. He was standing before me with a gentle look on his face. I opened my eyes and glanced around. Nothing seemed abnormal. I closed my eyes again. The man returned. He lifted his hand toward the scrape on my forehead. I flinched a little as his fingers moved close to my face, but I didn't stop him this time. His touch was warm and tender. He stroked my cheek and hair. His brilliant blue eyes gazed into mine.

"I'll protect you, Ysolde. Go to sleep," he said as he faded away.

Ysolde? He knows my name and said he would protect me. He must be the Lumen man. My body became warm and relaxed. I could hear the man's soothing voice echoing my name as I fell asleep.

7. Third Sight

Morning came way too early. My body jerked when my alarm clock went off. I hit the snooze and snuggled back under my comforter. At 7:05, the alarm blared again.

"Turn the damn thing off!" croaked Tiff, her voice muffled from somewhere deep within her pink cocoon.

"Okay, okay," I slapped the off button and sat up then gingerly touched my forehead. *Ouch* – not a good idea. My body was stiff and sore. I forced myself to get up and head to the bathroom.

Did all that really happen last night? The large scrape and bruise on my forehead was proof enough. I applied a ton of makeup to try to conceal the nasty-looking wound then combed my hair to the side to partially cover it up. My bathrobe was plush and warm. Mom had given it to me a few days before we drove to the canyon this summer. It had a faint smell of her perfume. I wrapped it closely around my body and walked back to the room.

Tiff was sound asleep. I drew the curtain back slightly and peeked out the window. The dawn sky was clear and crystal blue. The glass felt cold to my hand. I dressed in a grey stretch tee and jeans then pulled my brown alpaca sweater over my head, wincing as it stretched across my forehead. I put Athas in my pocket, pulled my knee boots on, grabbed my backpack then headed off to my 8:00 class, Environmental Biology.

By the time I found the correct classroom, the large, auditorium-style space was already packed. I had to walk down the stairs in front of everyone to the first row for an empty seat. It felt like all eyes were on me as I slithered into my spot. The professor checked roll, assigned everyone a number then handed out a lengthy syllabus and dismissed us to go buy our books.

I had a few hours before my next class. I headed to the cafeteria for breakfast, keeping my eyes on the trees and sky for anything unusual. Inside the building there were assorted students milling about. Some were rushing to class; most were visiting with others while mindlessly gazing at their phones. I walked toward the buffet.

Enlarged black and white photos of the canyon decorated the walls of the eating area. I tried to redirect my gaze, but they were enormous and everywhere. My eye caught one photo taken from the same overlook where my parents fell to their deaths. The angle of the picture accentuated the sheer drop of two-thousand feet down to the Dragon's Tongue River. My throat seized with pain. Tears welled in my eyes. I left the buffet line and hurried out the door. *I have to get a grip and control this.*

My appetite was gone. I walked over to the library next door to calm down. On the second floor, there was a lone chair tucked away in a private nook. The local newspaper was in the seat. I sat down and picked up the paper to read it. The headline said, "Death Canyon," with a large photo of the place where the girl was found dead.

The canyon was everywhere. I couldn't get away from it. It was as if something didn't want me to forget about my parent's deaths and the battle I faced ahead with Kraegon. I closed my eyes and tried to shut it all out, but knew that was impossible.

A little before 10:00, I left the library and walked to my Creative Writing class. All twelve students sat around one big table. Everyone was close enough to see the huge bruise on my forehead. Fortunately, the staring didn't last too long and no one asked any questions. The professor talked briefly about the syllabus, then let us leave early.

As I walked out of the English building I felt my cell phone buzz in my pocket. It was Cam. I couldn't imagine anyone I'd rather see right now. I needed to feel close to someone warm and supportive.

"Hey Cam! What's up?"

"Just wanted to see if you'd like to have an early lunch with me." Cam's voice sounded strong and cheerful.

"Sure, anywhere but the cafeteria."

"Okaaay. Should I ask?"

"I'll tell you later."

"I'm at the fountain near your dorm."

"See you there." My heart smiled. Lunch with Cam. My appetite just returned. Maybe today will be a good day after all.

I checked my phone for any messages from Dan. Nothing yet. *Of course.* I reached into my pocket making sure Athas was still safe then walked to the fountain.

As I approached Cam, his eyes stared at the goose egg on my forehead.

"What the hell happened to you?"

I couldn't tell him I had smashed into a tree running from an energy entity while in the woods alone last night.

"It's nothing, really. My roommate had this huge party in our room last night and I got a little carried away, so now I have this lovely souvenir," I grinned, proud of myself for coming up with such a plausible excuse on the fly.

"Looks pretty nasty. Did you fall?"

"I tripped and fell on my desk, head first. It looks worse than it is."

"I never took you for a party girl," Cam chuckled. I laughed with him as I tried to pull my hair a little more across my injury. "How was the party otherwise?"

"Lots of jocks and girls who want to hook up with jocks."

"That doesn't sound like you. I'm surprised you stuck around for it."

"Just trying to fit in, I guess," I shrugged, hoping he'd change the subject.

"So, did that make you want to date a big, hairy jock?" Did I detect a hint of jealousy? I could only wish.

"There was one guy who seemed eager to meet me. He was actually pretty good-looking, but I like a guy with a brain. I mean jocks have brains. You know what I mean."

Cam laughed. "I know what you're trying to say. Are you still a vegetarian?"

"Of course! That's not going to change." I'd been a vegetarian since I was twelve after watching a video about the extreme cruelty of factory farming, slaughterhouses and transporting animals in semi-trucks, not to mention the billions of dollars and thousands of acres it takes to raise animals to be eaten. All that money and land could be used to raise more healthy food from non-meat sources that would feed so many more people. I was normally not very political, but on this subject I held firmly to my beliefs and the facts.

"There's a cool little place off-campus around the corner you're gonna love," Cam said, pointing to the right.

We walked a few blocks to a natural foods café. Cam took me around back to an intimate brick patio eating area draped with flowering vines overhead. Gentle guitar music played in the background. It was heavenly. I exhaled, allowing myself to relax momentarily.

The menu was written on a chalk board placed on an easel near the back door. I ordered a toasted avocado and Swiss cheese on dark rye sandwich. Cam ordered a veggie burger. We ate and chatted about my morning on campus. At first Cam was light hearted and sweet, then his face fell and he grew silent.

"What's wrong?" I asked.

"There's been another girl found in the canyon, Ysolde." His voice was edgy and raw.

"*Another* one found dead?" My stomach cramped. I thought of my near encounter with the possible murderer last night.

"It was almost the identical scenario as before. She was alone on the rim. I know how you like to hike and camp, but you need to stay away from there."

"The canyon rim was where my parents – don't worry; I have no desire to go near there." I couldn't make myself tell Cam how they really died, how it wasn't an accident like everyone thought. Of all the people on the planet who would be sympathetic, he would be the most, but I just couldn't do it. I thought about my hiking date with Alia next Saturday. I'd have to make sure she took me seriously. There was no way she was going to talk me into hiking around the canyon.

"Don't even go into the woods," Cam said. "Promise me you won't do anything stupid. I told Dan I'd watch out for you, but I can't do that if you're way out there."

It was a little late for not doing something stupid. I took a bite of my sandwich and didn't respond.

"I mean it, Ysolde." Cam sounded more like Dan every minute. He stared at me, waiting for a promise I couldn't make. I swallowed and took a big swig of water, thinking of something to say.

I finally said, "This lunch has been great. You are so thoughtful. You have no idea how much I needed this little break, but I need to go back to the dorm before painting class. " I started to get up.

Cam touched my arm. "You're holding something back. I know you."

"I'm just a little tired from that party last night, that's all. Everything's fine, okay?"

"You'd tell me if something wasn't right, wouldn't you?"

"Of course I would," I smiled. "Thanks again for lunch. We should do it again soon."

"Count on it."

We both stood up and Cam gave me a hug then we went our separate ways. I walked back toward the campus feeling guilty for not telling him the truth. Without Oma to talk to, I had no one to confide in.

Intro to Painting was my last class of the day. I gathered my art supplies from the dorm room and walked to the art building. Instead of looking forward to my favorite subject, I dreaded going so close to the woods and that trail from hell from last night. I stood in front of the building, my eyes scanning the trees nearby.

"You going in or are you just admiring the scenery?" Cam said from behind me.

"Hey!" I smiled. "What are you doing here?"

"I'm taking this class, too."

"Really?"

"I needed an elective and since you were taking it, I thought why not. I wanted it to be a surprise," he grinned.

"This is great! You have perfect timing."

"Why do you say that?"

"I'm just glad you're here." This was too good to be true.

Cam opened the door for me. We entered a hallway then found the door to the painting studio. Chairs were informally arranged in a group for our first meeting. There were easels placed near the walls. A few already had paintings on them. The room had a heavy odor of paint, a smell I had grown to love.

Besides Cam and myself, there were seven other students in the room. They were a mix of eclectic types, considered misfits anywhere else but art class. The professor handed out a material's list and a schedule which required ten paintings by the end of the semester. Cam's eyes shifted to mine with a panicked, "What the hell?" look on his face. I patted him on the knee and gave him a reassuring smile.

Behind us, the door opened and a student silently entered the room. My body went from comfortably cool to extremely warm in seconds. My stomach clenched from the familiar feeling of last night. The student walked directly behind me. I felt a tingling run through my body like he was tickling my bare back with a huge feather. My posture became alert and straight. No one else seemed to be bothered. I glanced over my shoulder in his direction, trying to be nonchalant.

The student went to the back corner of the room, away from the group and sat alone. Cam leaned toward me, looking at the sweat on my forehead.

"Why are you sweating?" he said quietly.

"I'll be right back," I whispered.

I left the room and stood on the other side of the door for a moment. The symptoms began to subside slightly. Could this be the same guy from the woods? I waited a few minutes then opened the door and walked back in, looking in his direction. The heat and magnetism immediately came back. It must be him. *What is he doing in my class?*

The art professor finished his introduction and told everyone to claim one of the easels. I picked the one closest to the mystery guy.

I recognized his face immediately. He was the man from the woods. Even though it had been dark in the forest making it hard to see details, his white blonde hair and tall, lean body matched what I remembered. The sensations of warmth and his resemblance couldn't be a coincidence.

My heart raced. I tried not to stare, but I couldn't help it. Should I speak?

"Please move," he said coolly, staring out the window.

"What?" Wasn't this the guy who escorted me safely out of the forest, the one who said he'd protect me in my vision, the one who comforted me to sleep?

"There's a spot over there." He nodded his head toward the opposite corner of the room then shifted his gaze back to the window, tuning me out.

What is with the attitude? He had to be the same guy.

"Aren't you the guy who was in the woods last night?"

He totally ignored me. Energy entity or not, he didn't need to be so rude. I jerked my supplies up and moved across the room. As soon as I vacated my spot, a girl with purple striped hair and multiple facial piercings grabbed the space. I watched, expecting him to evict her as rapidly as he did me. To my amazement and great disappointment, the man completely ignored her.

Cam walked over to me. "Class is over, lover girl," he said sarcastically. "You spent the entire class staring at that guy."

"Sometimes I do stupid things," I admitted.

"Come on, let's get outta here."

I looked back at the man one last time as we neared the door. He turned away from the window and stared directly into my eyes. I ran right into Cam. We both stumbled our way out of the room.

"What is *wrong* with you?" he chuckled.

"I have no idea," I said in a fog, as we walked out of the building. "Do you know that guy?"

"Never saw him before. He looks a little older than your typical student."

"I think I may know him."

"Dammit, Ysolde! You need to be careful. He's kind of freaky looking."

"Calm down. It's not like I'm going to go hiking with him or anything." *Even though I'm pretty sure I did last night.*

"Excuse me for caring."

"Dan would be so proud of you," I grinned, patting him on the back. "I have to buy some books. Talk to you later?"

"Promise me you'll only talk to that guy in class, where it's safe? Or better yet, don't talk to him at all."

"I'll try."

"Ysolde . . ."

"Trust me," I said, as I walked away. *Now if I could only trust myself.*

8. FURIA

No word from Dan yet with a response from Oma. I sent him a text while standing in line at the bookstore. "HELLOOOOOOO?????" Still no response.

I knew I was about to do another stupid thing. If the man in my art class was the Lumen man, maybe he had to conceal his identity which might explain his attitude, although that didn't really make sense. I still didn't understand why he was in my class in the first place. If I went back to the painting studio tonight, maybe he would show up when I was alone and we could talk.

I could see one of those scenes in a horror film beginning to unfold. A girl is about to stupidly go outside into the dark where the murderer is, because she heard a noise or she's looking for someone who has disappeared. You know she's going to be brutally killed and you don't want to watch, but you watch anyway, because maybe she'll get lucky and survive. I was hoping I would be the girl who survives.

I needed the Lumen man's guidance and protection. I needed him to show me how to use this stone I had been protecting and carrying around everywhere at Oma's insistence. Why was he making this meeting so hard? Tonight, I would find out.

I ate a bite at the bookstore cafe then headed to the dorm. Tiff was out of the room. I freshened up and tried to calm my nerves. The sun dipped behind the mountains, casting a cold shadow on the campus. I walked back to the art building and saw that the lights were still on. The professor had told us the building would be open until midnight every night. No one was in the painting studio. I decided to start on my first assignment while I waited to see if the Lumen man would appear.

Our first project was to make a painting in any style on cardboard. The prof said the cardboard would keep us from taking our paintings too seriously as beginners. I missed doing my art and didn't care what I painted on. I chose the largest piece of cardboard in the stack and placed it on the floor then applied a coat of white primer.

While I waited for the primer to dry, I arranged my paints and brushes on my paint stand and poured a cup of water for my acrylics. I checked my text messages again from Dan. Nothing. *Dammit Dan! Come on!*

I sent him another text. "OMA??????"

When the primer dried, I placed the cardboard on my easel and stared at it, waiting for inspiration. Sometimes I would see lines or shapes appear on the surface which would give me a starting place. Not tonight. My mind was too consumed with worry and fear of the unknown.

I glanced across the room at the mystery man's area in the corner by the window. Maybe he had written his name on something. I walked to his easel. There were no supplies. The spot looked empty as if he'd never been there or had no intention of coming back.

Maybe I could dowse to see if he was the Lumen man. I removed the crystal pendant from my neck then took three breaths and tried to clear my mind. I held the crystal by the silver chain and asked, "Was the man who was sitting in this space during my class today, the Lumen Oma said would meet me?" The question was too awkward, but maybe the pendulum understood.

I watched as the pendulum swung back and forth as if trying to make up its mind, then it began to swing counter clockwise in a definite no response. Goosebumps ran down my arm. If he's not the Lumen man, who is he? *What* is he? Could Kraegon morph his appearance to look like the Lumen man?

"Was the man who was sitting in this spot today during my painting class *human*?"

The pendulum swung back and forth again in indecision then finally began swinging counter clockwise for another no response. He was not human. I was amazed that that information didn't faze me. A week ago I would have totally freaked out at the thought of anyone not being human. Who would have thought I'd get used to the idea of non-humans running around like it was normal? But still, the man was apparently not *the* Lumen I was waiting for. I needed more clarification.

I raised the crystal to ask another question then I saw a tall figure standing in the dark hall by the studio. I crammed the crystal into my pocket. The figure stepped into the doorway. It was the mystery man. Not only did he see me dowsing, but I was doing it in his space. I was mortified and speechless.

"What are you doing?" he asked. His tone was critical and direct. He seemed agitated. I lost my nerve to ask if he was the Lumen Oma spoke of. I needed to get out of there.

"I was just looking out the window for my friend and now I see him. I have to go," I said as I hurried over to my paint stand and grabbed my backpack. The man's piercing eyes followed. He didn't move from the door. I hesitated then pushed past him, averting my eyes from his gaze.

"Be careful," he said, suddenly sounding as if he cared again.

I ran down the hall and rammed the bar on the exit door, flinging it wide open. A strong cold energy blew through my skin as the heavy door slammed shut behind me. I stopped briefly to scan the area. The woods from last night were just a few yards away. Something leapt from behind a tree a few feet in front of me.

"Help!" I yelled, as I turned back to the door and jerked it open. The mystery man was standing on the other side. I was trapped. He grabbed my arm and pulled me inside the building.

"Stay here," he said then he bolted out the door.

Like hell stay here! I waited a few minutes then opened the door and looked out. I couldn't see anything. It looked safe for the moment. I had to make a run for it. I leapt out the door and ran back to the dorm, reliving last night all over again.

The mystery man had tried to help me. Maybe he was my guardian after all. *Who the hell knows?*

When I arrived at my room the door was locked. I started to use my key when I heard Tiff and Tanner groaning and giggling inside. I knocked on the door and waited impatiently. There was a loud thump like someone had fallen out of bed followed by hysterical laughter. A moment later the door cracked open and Tiff's flushed face peeked out. Her naked body was wrapped loosely in a pink blanket.

"Come back in an hour, k?" she whispered in a sexy, breathy voice, moving her tussled hair from her eyes.

"Where am I supposed to go?" *No more being nice!*

"Hurry baby, I don't have all night," Tanner whined in the background.

"Just one sec, sweetie." She turned back toward me and chirped, "You'll be fine." Then she quickly shut the door in my face.

Apparently, I had no backbone. I should've demanded that Tanner leave so I could get some sleep, but how do you defy the pink queen? I walked down the hall. Alia's door was open. She was sitting at her computer. I knocked and walked in.

"Hey," I said. Alia turned to face me.

"Hey, Ysolde. What's up?"

"Tiff and Tanner."

Alia snorted, "Say no more. I told you she was a major party girl. You're welcome to hang here if you want. Have a seat."

"Thanks." I sank into a blue bean bag chair and leaned my head back, staring at the ceiling. "Please don't feel like you have to talk to me. I mean, it feels nice just to sit and do nothing."

"You have to set limits with her or she'll run you out of the room every night," Alia said. "That's what she did with all her other roommates."

"I don't like confrontations."

"It wouldn't have to be a confrontation. But she needs to be reminded that you have just as much right as she does to be in there."

"Yeah, I know," I sighed. Why couldn't I be strong like Alia?

We chatted for a little while. Alia told me she was a local girl, but chose to live in the dorm to get away from her parents. I told her about Texas, but couldn't bring myself to tell her about my parent's deaths. After about an hour I walked down the hall to see if my room was clear. The door was still locked. I didn't have the energy to knock and deal with Tiff again, even though I wanted to kick the door down and throw them both out.

Alia offered a sleeping bag on the floor for the night. I said yes. Sleeping on the floor was better than nothing. I'd deal with the roommate situation later.

I was so tired that the cold, hard floor in a sleeping bag in my clothes was minor. Alia gave me one of her pillows. I checked my phone for messages one last time. Still nothing. Dan was going to get an earful from me tomorrow. I put the phone on the floor beside me and fell asleep soon after Alia turned the lights off.

When I woke up, it was early morning. Alia was still asleep. I quietly gathered my shoes and phone and crept out of the room. My door was no longer locked. I went inside. Tanner was gone. Tiff didn't budge from underneath her puffy comforter. The stuffed animals were strewn about the room, banished by the pink queen so she could have her way with the pink king.

It was 6:00 a.m. My class was starting at 9:00. I had enough time to take a nap in a real bed. I set my alarm for 8:00, undressed and burrowed into my nest. My little bed felt like home for the first time, even if the bras from the party were still hanging from the ceiling.

My first class of the day was Medieval Art History. Some of my father's ancestors had been traced back to the medieval times in the Black Forest of Germany. I was looking forward to learning more about art from that area. The professor gave an introduction to the class with an assignment of chapters to read.

I had an hour before my next class. I went to the bookstore cafe and bought a cup of hazelnut coffee and a cinnamon bagel. I called Dan. His phone went to voicemail again. I left a flaming message.

Not long afterwards, I began to feel dizzy. A cold chill raced down my spine. I turned in my chair and looked around. My eyes scanned the students and buildings. The dizziness turned to nausea. I jumped up and ran behind a large bush nearby, ready to expel my bagel.

I knelt under the bush in the leaves and debris. Then the dizziness vanished and my chills turned to warm sweat. The mystery man had to be near. Even though the pendulum had said he was not the one I was supposed to meet, he had to be connected in some way. I looked around for the tall, good-looking guy with the white hair as the feeling continued to grow in intensity.

A warm hand suddenly touched my back, startling me. I jerked around and saw Cam's friendly face.

"What are you doing in the bushes?" he chuckled.

I had to think of something quick. I grabbed a crushed soda can half buried under the dirt and held it up.

"I'm picking up trash, see?"

"Gross."

"No kidding." I wiped my fingers on my jeans and crawled out from under the bush. "What's up?"

"I'm on my way to the archaeology lab. And you're on litter patrol?" he laughed.

"Not really. What time is it?"

Cam looked at his phone. "10:45."

"Oh, wow. I have class in fifteen minutes. Sorry, I gotta go!"

I left Cam standing there staring at me like I was nuts. I didn't know what I was doing. Should I go to class or skip it? I walked toward my government class, taking deep breaths, while scanning the trees and faces around me. The feeling of heat slowly began to dissipate. It seemed every time I felt the cold nausea, the warm sensations would soon overtake them. I was beginning to see a pattern. Cold then warm. Vapor then Lumen?

In government class, the professor didn't let us go early like my other profs had this week. Somehow I managed to stay awake through the hour of his monotone ramblings. After class I walked back to the dorm.

My room was empty with no Tiff or Tanner. It was a good time to finish unpacking. I opened the box with my personal computer and printer and set them on my desk. I hooked all the wires and cables up then eagerly logged on to the online game Dan and I played. In our game, we preferred player-versus-player. Furia was my paladin. Wolfbane was Dan's warrior. Furia wore heavy armor, swung a two-handed sword and could heal in a pinch. She was strong and fearless. I liked to think she was my alter ego.

To my surprise, Dan was logged in. Furia sent Wolfbane an in-game message.

"Heya! Whaddup?" Furia said.

"Heya!" Wolfbane responded.

"Got pc hooked up."

"I see that. How's it going?"

"Why don't you answer my texts?" Furia asked.

"Haven't checked lately."

"No kidding!!!! I need a response from Oma, asap."

"About?"

"The man?"

"Oh yeah. Just a sec."

A few minutes passed then Wolfbane returned.

"Oma says you'll know," Wolfbane said.

"What??"

"You'll. Know."

"No. I won't! What is the man's *name?*" Furia shrieked with impatience.

A few more minutes passed. "Oma says his name is Von," said Wolfbane. My heart stopped.

Von – from the canyon Von? I couldn't ask Dan that. He wasn't supposed to know about any of this. I recalled on the day my parent's died, Oma had seen someone or something in the sky she called "Von."

I needed to dowse to find out.

"So, you wanna play?" asked Wolfbane.

"Sure. Give me a minute."

I took my necklace off and held it in front of me. When I dowsed in the studio, the pendulum said the mystery man wasn't human and he wasn't the Lumen man Oma was talking about. I had to ask again, but in a different way.

"Is the *entity* that was alone in the art building with me last night named Von?"

The pendulum immediately began swinging clockwise for yes. For some reason the pendulum hadn't considered him Lumen or human when I asked before, maybe because he seemed to be both. Regardless of the reasoning, Von was the Lumen Oma said would be my guardian and would help me. Why was he being so secretive?

I glanced back at the computer screen. Wolfbane was jumping up and down and dancing with Furia, waiting for her to play with him.

I loved fantasy and science fiction, but now it was real. Too real. I didn't want this new life. I wanted to play and go back to happier times. I put the pendant back around my neck.

"Got ganked by an asshole before you logged on," Wolfbane snarled. "Come on. Let's teach him a lesson."

"On my way," declared Furia as she mounted her glowing winged stallion and flew alongside Wolfbane on his shining black dragon.

I was lost in the total bliss of in-game role-playing and the distraction from real life. We caught up with the player who had attacked Wolfbane and gave him a good thrashing then played in the battlegrounds, slashing and slamming our way to victory. Every player I attacked was victim to my frustration and anger that had been building inside me since my parent's deaths. I could've played for hours, shutting out the world I wanted so desperately to ignore, then Tiff and Tanner showed up. I knew what was coming. I reluctantly told Wolfbane goodbye and logged out.

"Whatcha doin?" Tiff asked, as she pawed Tanner's shirt off.

"Playing a game."

"Oh my God. You're a geek!" she laughed.

"Yep, that's me," I sighed, shutting the computer off. I grabbed my jacket and backpack and headed out the door. "Have fun," I mumbled.

I didn't see Von for the rest of the week. Wednesday, Thursday and Friday classes came and went without any unexpected surprises. I painted a preliminary idea on my cardboard for art class. Cam was still struggling with an idea for his painting.

I wanted to assume all was well with the Lumen and maybe Von had gone back to wherever he had come from. The hot and cold sensations I'd been having had not returned. Maybe my life was going to be normal after all — but I knew better.

Friday night, Tiff and Tanner were having their usual rendezvous in my room. I found the student union building was a good place to hang out during their sessions. I convinced myself I could live with that. Deep inside, I felt like a whipped dog. Little did I know I'd never have to worry about confronting Tiff and Tanner again.

9. Deja Vu

I woke around 3:00 a.m. on a couch in the student union building. Would I ever get to spend an entire night in my bed? I pushed my hair out of my face, put my jacket on and walked back to the dorm.

The door to my room was unlocked. That usually meant Tanner was gone. It was Saturday. Finally, I could catch up on my sleep.

As I entered, I saw Tiff lying in an awkward position on the floor in her pink bunny pajamas. She must've pulled a doozy last night. Her left hand clasped the corner of her pink comforter pulled halfway off the bed. Her mouth was wide open, like a suffocated fish out of water.

I lay my backpack on the bed and knelt beside her.

"Tiff? You okay?" No response. I touched her face. Her skin was cold and pale. Her eyes were glazed over. Drug overdose immediately ran through my mind.

"Tiff! Wake up!" I shouted, pulling her head and shoulders into my arms. Her body was heavy and flimsy. I slapped her face. Her head fell backwards. I grabbed her upper body and shook it. There was no response. Stuffed animals around the room stared at me with wide, curious eyes.

I felt for a pulse. There was no sign of life. Could she be dead? My breath quickened. I'd never seen a dead person. My eyes scanned the room looking for clues. There were no signs of violence or a struggle. I gently laid her head back down on the floor then leaped out of the room, screaming for help.

Nearly everyone on my floor was standing in the hall in front of my room when the paramedics and police arrived. I sat on my bed trying to answer the multitude of questions the officials asked. Tiff was dead. I barely knew her. Could she have been murdered?

"Where's Tanner?" I asked one of the girls in the doorway.

"Who's Tanner?" the policeman asked.

"He's Tiff's boyfriend," I said.

"What's his last name?" He began writing on a pad.

"I don't know. I just met him this week. There's no way he did this."

"You might be surprised," said the officer.

The detectives asked me to leave the room so they could investigate, but not to leave the dorm. I pushed my way through the crowd of weeping girls down to Alia's room to spend the remaining few hours before dawn. I lay on the floor in her sleeping bag, wide awake.

Around 6:00 a.m., the coroner took Tiff's body away. I had nodded off, but woke when I heard the residence hall director crying. When I walked back to my room the crowds of girls were gone and the hall was empty except for a few police outside my door. They said it was okay for me to leave the dorm now, but to expect detectives in my room for the next several days. The police let me in briefly to collect toiletries and clothes for the weekend. I learned that Tanner had never shown up and was now wanted for questioning.

Death had become the theme of my life. How could Tiff be dead? How could my mom and dad be dead? Those two girls who died couldn't be a coincidence. All the deaths were centered around Abysmal. This place was evil. Maybe it *was* Kraegon who had killed my parents and the girls in the canyon. And Tiff? Would he kill her to get to me? If only I could talk to Oma. She would tell me what to do next. I needed Dan. I had Cam, but I couldn't tell him about Kraegon. I needed Von to return and help me understand what was going on *if he would just talk to me*. I felt lost and abandoned. My eyes burned with tears.

I looked like hell in the mirror, but didn't care. I took a quick shower and dressed in the bathroom then returned to Alia's room. She was awake.

"Morning," I said softly.

"You think Tanner did it?" she asked.

"I don't know. I never heard him argue with Tiff. He seemed like a big, horny teddy bear."

"They did seem pretty close, but I can't imagine who else it could've been."

"I have no idea," I lied. There was no way I was telling Alia about Kraegon.

"Do you still want to go hiking today?" she asked. "My friends and I are still going. They didn't know Tiff."

I'd forgotten about our hiking date. It had been less than an hour since Tiff's body had been removed by the coroner. Hiking or doing anything fun seemed insensitive as well as the fact that Kraegon was probably out there somewhere, just waiting for me.

"I'm not sure that's such a good idea. I mean, what if the police need to ask me more questions?"

"Did they say you had to stick around?"

"No, they said I could leave. I don't know, it still feels disrespectful to Tiff."

"This whole thing is crazy."

"Yeah." I stared out the window at the cloudless morning sky. My mind flashed back to Tiff's dead face in my arms.

"Come on. Tiff wouldn't want you to hang around here and be sad. If the tables were turned and you had died, she'd probably throw a party," Alia laughed.

"You're probably right." Alia had no idea how easily it could have been me instead of Tiff lying stone cold dead on the floor.

"Do it in her honor."

"I don't know."

"The fresh air would do you good," she persisted.

I thought about how the forest used to rejuvenate my spirit – but that was before Kraegon. Still, what was I going to do all day? Stay in the dorm and listen to everybody cry?

"Well, the fresh air *would* do me good." *What was I saying?* There were multiple reasons I shouldn't go, my life being one of them.

"Great! Except, my car's dead. Can you drive?

"Yeah, okay."

"Cool. We've got about an hour before we meet my friends."

"I'm going to see if I can stay at Cam's this weekend," I said.

"You sure? You're welcome to stay here."

"He'll say yes." At least I was hoping Cam would say yes. Sleeping in my clothes on the hard floor at Alia's was getting old. I couldn't imagine sleeping in my room, surrounded by Tiff's lingering spirit; her orphaned stuffed animals staring at me with mournful eyes.

"Let's grab a bite to eat before we go," said Alia.

I went back to my room and put my jacket and hiking boots on and Dan's baseball cap he had given me. I checked my pocket making sure Athas was safe. Alia and I walked to the cafeteria. I took one step inside, saw the canyon photos and walked out. Alia followed me back outside.

"What's wrong?" I knew she'd think my aversion to the photos was stupid. I had to think of something else.

"I can't stand that smell."

"What smell? Bacon?" she laughed. "I thought everybody loved bacon."

"Not me. I'm really not very hungry. I'm going to the student union building for some snacks and bottled water. I'll meet you back here in about thirty minutes, okay?"

"Okay, whatever." I could tell by her tone she thought I was weak.

After I left the snack bar, I called Cam. It took no persuading on my part for him to say yes to let me stay at his place. He was extremely concerned about Tiff's death and the situation in the dorm. He immediately connected her death with the other two that had occurred this week.

"I'm going away for the weekend so you'll have the place to yourself," he said.

"Where are you going?" My voice was elevated. I needed Cam to be with me this weekend. I was feeling lonely for the first time in my life.

"There's an archeology dig about fifty miles west of here. You'll be okay, right?"

"I guess. I was just hoping you'd be there." Dammit. That sounded clingy.

"Sorry. The dig is required for my class."

"That's okay. When will you be back?"

"Sometime tomorrow afternoon. The key is under the concrete pig by the back porch. Just make yourself at home and keep the doors locked."

"Thanks for this."

"No problem. I'll see you Sunday."

"See you then."

"Be careful," he added before hanging up.

I'm trying. But being careful doesn't seem to be part of the equation lately.

I met Alia in front of the cafeteria then we went to the parking lot to meet her friends. Two guys and a girl were crammed in the front seat of a white pickup with rusted holes on the sides and a cracked windshield.

"Mornin'," Alia said to them. "This is Ysolde."

The guy in the driver's seat looked at me through dark sunglasses. "Hey, I'm Jon. This is Jesse and Mags."

The other two glanced my way and smiled. I felt a cold tingling sensation run down my spine. The three in the truck looked like normal humans. I scanned the parking lot and didn't see anything. I didn't know who or what to trust anymore.

"You guys ready?" Alia asked.

"Born ready," Jon said. "Follow me," he shouted from his truck window as he drove away.

Alia and I followed the white truck up the narrow winding highway to the trail head about twenty miles from campus. On the way, we passed a national park sign that read "Abysmal Canyon, North Rim."

"Alia, I thought you said we weren't hiking near the canyon." My stomach suddenly tied in knots at the thought of the black, cavernous opening in the ground up ahead.

"Yeah, that was the original plan, but Jon and the others want to hike there. Their morbid sense of curiosity has gotten the better of them," she chuckled.

"But, I told you I didn't want to."

"Oh, don't be such a wuss, Ysolde. Jon's hiked all over this canyon. He knows the dangerous spots and besides, none of us are suicidal, are we?" She looked at me with a raised eyebrow and a wicked smile.

I sighed and stared out the windshield at the back of Jon's white truck ahead. Extreme anger was building inside me; anger over not having the nerve to stand up to people like Alia or Tiff, even though I couldn't be mad at Tiff now. Flashbacks of the rim crumbling and taking my parents to their deaths hovered mercilessly in my mind.

Jon's truck slowed and pulled over to the side of the road in a turn out area. I pulled up beside him and turned the Jeep off.

"I'm not staying," I said to Alia, trying to sound strong, but my voice cracked.

"You're such a baby," she laughed, sounding more like my nemesis than a friend. "If you're really that worried about it, I'll talk to Jon and see what he thinks."

She had no idea what I'd been through. So what if I sounded like a whiney baby? Furia, in the game, would never back down from hiking around the canyon. "Bring it!" would be her answer. But this was reality and I was truly afraid. I was convinced that the next victim was going to come from this group if we hiked in this location and that person would probably be me. Oma had warned me to pay particular attention to my gut feelings, and they were screaming to turn around and leave. I should never have come. *What was wrong with me?*

We walked over to Alia's friends.

"Thought we'd hike to the bottom of the canyon. I want to see where those girls died," Jon said. My eyes shifted to Alia.

"Sounds great!" Mags said, eagerly jumping over next to Jon, an obvious sign of possession. Alia looked back at me and shrugged. I glared at her.

She rolled her eyes then said, "Umm, Jon. Ysolde's not sure going down into the canyon is such a good idea."

All eyes were on me. Yes, I'm a wimp. Deal with it.

"What are you so worried about? No one's going to hurt us. I thought girls from Texas were gutsy," Jon said, winking at me.

"I have my reasons."

I should have gotten in my Jeep right then and headed back to the dorm. Alia and her daredevil friends could spend the entire weekend at the canyon of death if they wanted to.

"Alia, *you're* not afraid, are you?" asked Jon, taunting her.

"Me? Hell no! But, I invited Ysolde on this hike and I guess if she doesn't want to go then . . ."

"Come on, Ysolde. Where's your sense of adventure?" Jesse said.

I shook my head and looked down at my boots. All I wanted was to go for a nice little hike somewhere for some badly needed stress relief. I sure as hell didn't need all this drama, especially from Alia who had given the impression she wanted to be my friend, up until now. So much for that.

Alia sighed, "Sorry guys. I guess I'll have to stay here with her. You go ahead."

"Don't stay on my account, Alia. Why don't you go with them? There's no point in you not having a good time with your friends." I wanted to leave in peace, alone.

"No, I'll stay with you. After all, I did promise."

Well, damn.

Jon frowned. "Suit yourself. Don't wait up. When you're ready to leave, just go. This will take us most of the day." He jerked his pack out of the truck bed, obviously ticked off.

"Hey, don't be angry. I'll go down with you guys another time," Alia said.

"Whatever." Jon turned and started hiking rapidly toward the rim. Mags and Jesse caught up with him.

"Watch out for the Boogey Man!" Mags yelled back at me, laughing as she headed down the canyon trail. I didn't like Alia's friends and even my friendship with Alia was becoming debatable.

"Well, where do you want to hike?" Alia asked, looking at me like I was a big pain in the ass. God I hated this.

"Somewhere away from here."

"I really don't want to get back in the car and go somewhere else. We've wasted enough time. Why not hike up here on top of the canyon? We can stay away from the rim."

"No, Alia."

"Look, it's an easy hike. And if there *is* somebody out there who means us harm, he'll be easy to see. If we hike in the woods, we won't be able to see anyone until they're right on us because of the trees."

She did have a point. I remembered how hard it had been to see Kraegon in the trees. But he would've been hard to see anyway. We're talking about invisible entities. No. I had to stay firm.

"No. I'm leaving. You can go catch up with your friends." I turned toward the Jeep. Alia caught my arm.

"Come on, Ysolde. I'm sorry. I didn't really want to hike down the canyon with them. Let's just go for a short walk up here then go back to the dorm. How about it?"

I was tired. It seemed the only way to get back to the dorm was to agree to a short hike.

"Only if we stay away from the rim and stop at the first bend in the trail," I demanded.

"No problem."

I felt a strong tingling sensation in my back jeans pocket. I pulled Athas out for reassurance. Could the stone be warning me?

"Whatcha got there?" Alia said, looking at the shining black stone.

"Just a worry stone," I lied, realizing I shouldn't have pulled it out of my pocket in front of her.

"Can I see it?" Alarms went off in my mind. *No! Don't let her touch the stone!* Oma said protect Athas at all cost.

"It's just a rock." I pulled Athas close to my body.

"Let me touch it."

"It's just a plain old stone, Alia."

"There must be something special about it."

"It's been in my family for a long time."

"That's cool. Let me see it."

She suddenly jumped toward me and snatched the stone from my hand.

"Hey!" I tried to grab it back. She turned away.

"Relax. I'll give it back. I just want to look at it."

She caressed the stone's smooth surface, tracing the lines with her finger.

"What are these lines?"

"Give it back," I warned.

Alia pulled Athas closer; her eyes fixated on the marks. I felt a panic rise in my heart.

"Can I carry it for good luck today?" she joked.

"It wouldn't work for you."

I tried to grab Athas from her grip. She raised the stone into the air, out of my reach.

"So, what makes *this* stone so special? Better tell me soon or I'll cast it over the edge."

She started walking toward the rim.

"What the hell are you doing?" I shouted, grabbing her by the shoulder from behind. "Give it to me!" I screamed.

She laughed and handed Athas back.

"Calm down. Geez. I was only kidding. Never saw anyone care so much for a plain old rock."

I shoved Athas into my pocket.

"Like I said, it's been in my family a long time."

"And the crystal around your neck?"

"A gift from my grandmother." I put my hand on the pendant and took several steps back.

"You must come from a long line of rock hounds," she snickered.

"Something like that."

A bead of sweat rolled down my forehead. I wanted to leave without Alia. She could live or die out here. I didn't care at this point. This was a nightmare.

"Ready to hike?" she asked.

I stood silent for a few minutes, trying to repress my anger. Hiking was the last thing I wanted to do now.

"You go first." I didn't want her behind me. I didn't trust her.

"Okay, follow me." She boldly stepped ahead and started up the trail at a brisk pace.

I watched as her strong legs carried her effortlessly along. I envied her strength. She glanced back at me.

"You coming?"

"Slow down a bit."

She waited for a few minutes then bolted forward again.

It didn't take long for the high elevation to get to me. My breathing was coming in short, rapid bursts. I stopped to sit down in the dirt, pulling gulps of air into my aching lungs.

"Wait!" I shouted toward Alia between breaths. She continued hiking until I couldn't see her anymore. So much for the short hike. She wasn't my friend. I didn't know what she was.

I took a long drink from my water bottle and looked around to see if there were any other hikers in the area. The winding, narrow trail was deserted. I glanced toward the rim. My eyes began to sting. I hadn't been back to the canyon since the accident.

Something suddenly began to draw my body toward the mouth of the chasm. The sensation was seductive and magnetic. I stood up and started walking like a robot on command with no mind of my own. The force pulled me closer and closer to the rim. No matter how hard I tried not to walk, I couldn't stop.

Gusts of wind blew strands of hair across my face. A Peregrine falcon swooped past. Her wing feathers grazed my cheek. I watched as she aimed straight down into the abyss then disappeared. My heart pounded with memories.

I was pulled along the path until I found myself standing at the edge. I leaned back, trying desperately to fight the urge to step into the vaporous rift. Pointed black teeth emerged from a silver mist rising up from the river. The rushing water whipped back and forth like a writhing snake.

One of my boots nudged halfway off the rim. Energy coming up from the bottom of the canyon was a numbing cold; a sinister form that made me feel weak and dizzy. I tried to step away. My boot continued to inch forward. I had a flashback of the dream with the man at the canyon. I could see his face smiling as he beckoned me to step off the edge with him. I teetered back and forth, trying to keep from falling. My vertigo increased. Everything around me was spinning. An invisible force grabbed my shoulders and pulled me down toward the river. My knees buckled and my weight shifted forward. Everything went black as I fell helplessly into the canyon's widening jaws.

"Stop!" I heard a strong male voice echo against the sheer walls, but it was too late. I was descending into the black. I swung my arms wildly trying to grab thin air, my eyes filled with terror. Just like my parents, I was falling to my death.

10. VON

A warm rush suddenly came over my body, replacing the icy bolts of energy that were pulling me downward into the abyss. A bright light flashed then something gripped my chest. It pulled me upwards with extreme speed then shoved me back onto the canyon rim. For a brief moment, I thought I saw Von's face right before I collapsed onto the ground.

"Hey! Are you okay?" Alia yelled from up the trail. She ran back toward me.

"Did you see what just happened?" I asked.

"You were standing next to the rim then you fell to your knees, like you were about to faint or something. Must be the elevation getting to you."

I pulled my water bottle out of my pack and took a drink, still dazed. "You didn't see anyone or any*thing* weird in the canyon?"

Alia laughed. "There's nobody out here, Ysolde."

Something had pulled me off the edge into the canyon. That was not my imagination. And something had pulled me back to safety. That was *definitely* not my imagination. The whole experience was impossible and yet it happened. It had to be Kraegon trying to kill me to get Athas. And Von must have been the force that kept me from falling.

Just like the day the rim collapsed, killing my parents, Von somehow forced me back away from the edge. I could still feel his warm presence in my heart.

I checked my pocket for Athas. My fingertips felt the smooth, warm stone secure in its nest.

A faint sound of voices travelled up the trail behind me. I glanced toward the parking lot. A group of hikers were unloading their gear from their car. I was thankful we were no longer alone, but Alia was clearly disappointed.

"Damn, looks like we've got company. Let's get out of here. I'll drive. You've had enough for one day," Alia said.

"I'll be fine. I'll drive." I wasn't about to give her control of my Jeep. We hiked to the Jeep and drove back to the campus in silence.

When we arrived at the dorm, the police allowed me to enter my room briefly. Tiff's stuffed animals watched with lonely eyes as I gathered more clothes, toiletries, my laptop and a few books for the weekend at Cam's house. I stared at the spot on the carpet where I had found Tiff. Death was becoming an all too familiar, unwanted feeling. I grabbed a handful of pink tissues and hurried out the door, eager to get to Cam's house, away from the campus, the canyon and Alia.

Cam's house was the last house on a quiet dead end that overlooked a small mountain river. The roughhewn cedar homes on the street had a settled, natural look among the mature pines and colorful wild flowers that grew in the yards.

I walked around to the back of the house and retrieved the key from under the concrete pig then went inside. The interior was rustic, cozy and simple. A small kitchen shared the same space with the living room. In the corner was a wood burning stove. There were two bedrooms and one bath on the main floor and a tiny bedroom in the loft where Cam had said I could stay.

The only furniture in the loft was a single mattress on a metal frame with a wooden crate for a bed stand. A candle on a ceramic stand and a box of matches lay on the crate for a source of light. Cam had put fresh sheets and a blanket on the bed. A small window above the bed opened out into the upper boughs of an elder pine tree. A purple bedspread-sized drape with a black dragon hung from the ceiling down to the railing of the loft, as a makeshift wall for privacy. I felt right at home.

It was late afternoon. I made sure all the windows and doors were locked then took a quick shower. The hot water eased my tense muscles, but I couldn't relax. My mind was racing with anxiety about Tiff's death and what had happened at the canyon today. I dried off and dressed in clean jeans and a sweater. Cam had left assorted cereals and cans of vegetable soup on the kitchen counter for me. I poured a bowl of cereal and sat down on the couch in front of the sliding glass doors, looking out on the back deck.

I thought about Von when he came to me in the woods the night I hiked behind the art building and the night in the studio. I unclasped my pendant and dowsed to see if he was the one who stopped me from falling to my death in the canyon today. The pendulum swung clockwise for yes.

I put the pendant around my neck and leaned back on the couch. Both my mind and body were exhausted. Cam's house seemed safe. I closed my eyes and fell asleep. An image began to form in my mind. The blurry vision grew larger then suddenly cleared. It was Von. He reached toward me and stroked my cheek.

"Ysolde," Von's low voice whispered. I breathed deeply as he gently caressed my neck and pulled his fingers lightly through my hair.

"Open your eyes," he said.

I didn't want to open my eyes. Von's touch was hypnotic.

"Open your eyes, Ysolde," he repeated, this time touching my shoulder and pulling me forward.

I reluctantly opened my eyes. Von's image vanished. The house had grown dark. I stood up and found a light switch on the wall. When I flipped it on, a man with white hair and brilliant blue eyes was sitting on the couch staring at me. It was Von.

I stumbled backwards and reached into my pocket for Athas for reassurance. The stone wasn't there. It must still be in my other jeans on the floor of the bathroom. I felt sick. How could I have forgotten it? I had begun to believe the stone really did have magic powers. Without it I was weak and vulnerable. I started to tremble.

"It's okay, Ysolde," Von said. "I didn't mean to frighten you."

"How did you get in here?"

He smiled. "I am Von, the man your grandmother told you about."

"I know who you are, even though I had to figure it out for myself."

I walked over toward the back door and unlocked it in case I needed an escape route. I didn't think Von was there to hurt me, but I couldn't assume anything anymore.

"Why have you waited so long to tell me? Why didn't you tell me sooner, like in the woods or the studio or the canyon? I've been going through hell wondering what's going on."

"It has been hard for you," he said softly.

"Hard for *me*? My mom and dad are dead. My roommate is dead. I nearly died more than once. I'm all alone in this. You have no idea what I've been going through waiting for you to help me and now you finally decide to introduce yourself, scaring me half to death?"

"I'm sorry. I had my reasons for waiting to tell you. You have not been alone. I haven't left your side since your arrival at Abysmal."

"Were you at the canyon today?"

"Yes. Kraegon tried to kill you to take the stone. Athas must be attuned to you tonight, then Kraegon cannot use it, as long as you are alive."

"As long as I'm alive?"

"If you die, one of Kraegon's human minions can take the stone and attune it. Kraegon will then have the ability to enter the positive energy lines and destroy the Lumen, destroy the world within and, in turn, destroy Earth. This is why I guard you with my life. We cannot delay. Where is the stone?"

I hurried to the bathroom. My dirty jeans still lay on the floor. I pushed my hand deep into my pocket, and to my horror, Athas was gone.

11. COMMITMENT

I panicked and dropped to my knees to look for the stone. I searched under my clothes, the bath mat, behind the toilet, in the shower. Did I take Athas out of my pocket and put it in my backpack?

Von appeared in the bathroom doorway. His shadow filled the tiny space. I backed into the corner, looking up at his solemn face. He grasped my left hand firmly. Electric vibrations shot up my arm. His glaring eyes were almost glowing. He was angry. I could feel it.

"I'm sorry, I . . ."

"Never leave Athas unguarded again," he said as he placed the stone in my palm. "This is not a game, Ysolde. The lives of many rest in your hands."

I knew Athas wasn't just a mere stone, but the sudden acceptance of the reality of the moment was too much for me to handle. I couldn't breathe. I bolted past Von through the living room then out the sliding glass doors. Gasping for air, I leaned over the porch railing overlooking the river.

Von followed me. I felt the warmth of his presence as he approached from behind. I was so conflicted. I wanted him to go away. I wanted all of this to go away. But I needed him. I needed my guardian.

"I won't let you die, Ysolde. I will give my life to protect you."

Lightning flashed above the mountains. Subtle sounds of thunder rolled across the sky. The wind picked up. I stared down at the river watching the water glisten in the intermittent moonlight as clouds rushed overhead. My mind slipped into silent mode. No words were necessary or welcome. No words could change my life now.

Von stood next to me, quietly staring into the distance, respecting my need for silence. My previous life of freedom had morphed into a bizarre life of great responsibility, a responsibility I did not want but seemed to have no control over. Like a wild horse that had been caught, my spirit was racing around the corral looking for a way to escape.

After a time, Von spoke.

"You must accept your fate, Ysolde. You won't be alone. I will always be with you. It's time to attune the stone."

I drew in a breath and opened my hand to look at Athas.

"Did your grandmother teach you about the energy lines in the ground?" he asked.

I nodded silently. Von took my other hand.

"Come to the river with me." He gently pulled me along. I walked with him down the porch steps. We hiked down the steep embankment to the river's edge. The rushing water was pulsing with life.

"Can you find a positive energy line along the bank?" he asked.

I unclasped my pendant to dowse for the line.

"No, Ysolde, not with your crystal." Von took the pendant from my hands and secured it back around my neck. His light touch caressed the nape of my neck. Chills ran down my spine. He leaned down and whispered in my ear, "Dowse with your body."

Oma had tried to teach me the basics of dowsing with my body with no pendulum. It required tremendous concentration. I had failed at every attempt.

I shook my head. "I can't body dowse. I've tried and I was a miserable failure."

Von put his hands on my shoulders. His eyes were sparkling as if they had a life of their own.

"You must trust yourself. You know what energy feels like. You felt it in the canyon. You felt it in the woods. You feel it every time I touch you, don't you?"

"Yes, but . . ."

He continued. "First you must focus, then with each step, you must pay close attention to the slightest sensations in your body, especially your fingertips, your palms and your feet.

"This is a waste of time. I know I can't do this," I said as I began walking at a steady pace down the river bank.

"Go slower. Walk in slow motion," Von said. "You must give yourself time to feel. Stay in each spot for a few moments before moving."

I tried walking in slow motion, stopping at each step to listen to my body. The only sensations I felt were the wind blowing through my hair and the cold air rising from the frigid water.

"Take your boots off," he said. "It will be easier to feel the electromagnetic current barefoot."

"My boots? The water is freezing!"

Von looked at me with just a hint of a smile. I knew he was right. Oma said dowsing barefoot always gave the best results. I yanked my boots off and continued walking. The sharp stones jabbed into the tender soles of my feet, making it nearly impossible to concentrate.

After I had walked about one hundred feet in what seemed an eternity, I took one more step and suddenly felt a slight warm tingling in my left hand. My breath quickened. Was it my imagination or maybe just a random nerve response that meant nothing? I took another step forward and the feeling stopped. I stepped back and the sensation returned.

"I think I found one!" I called down river to Von.

"I was wondering when you'd find it," he replied calmly, walking toward me.

"You knew where it was?"

He chuckled softly, like Dan used to do when I'd said something obvious and dumb. I hated feeling stupid.

"Stand on the energy line and take a step to one side," he said. I stepped to the right.

"I still feel it."

"Good. Now take a few steps to the left."

I took a few steps. "Yes, it's still there."

116

"That's the direction of the energy line. It's not running in front or behind you, but from left and right of you. Now hold the stone in your palm. One of the lines is wider than the other."

I felt the two lines and could easily sense the difference between the wide line and the thinner one.

"The wider line is for positive energy. Align that with where you are standing, like this." Von turned the stone to the proper alignment in my hand. I felt a surge of electric current.

"Did you feel anything?"

"Yes! Like sparks running through my body."

"Excellent. The line on the stone and the energy line are now in tune. Turn the stone clockwise slowly and don't stop until I tell you to."

I turned the stone in small increments. The space around me started to warp, waving back and forth. I felt dizzy and started to fall back. Von stood behind me, his hands steadying my body.

"Hold on a little longer," he said.

"I'm going to faint."

"Don't worry, I've got you. It gets easier with time."

A few feet beyond me, an oval-shaped hole about five feet tall appeared in midair. It was filled with millions of tiny lights and began to pull me toward it.

"Help! What's it doing?" Von grabbed my waist and held me back.

"We're not going in yet. Turn the stone in the opposite direction."

I turned the stone counter-clockwise. The pulling stopped and the vortex closed. Von caught me in his arms as I fell back.

"I think I'm going to throw up." I sat down in the grass by the water's edge. The warping slowly began to subside.

"You did well. You'll get used to it. Now look at the other side of the stone."

I turned the stone over. In the moonlight, I could see numerous lines etched into the stone on the side that used to be bare.

"When did that happen?"

"Those are the lines from your palm. They are a unique blueprint of your soul. Athas has accepted you. You and the stone are one now."

Von knelt on one knee before me like someone who is about to propose. He bowed his head.

"My lady, Domina Lumen, I vow to serve only you. Will you accept me as your guardian?"

For most girls who lived a normal life, having a chivalrous, handsome man kneel in front of them asking if he could be their guardian would be a fantasy come true. But, this wasn't a fantasy. This was as serious as it gets. Athas was attuned to me now. I was the Domina Lumen, whether I liked it or not. I needed Von. He was not only my guardian, but my mentor as well. What I wanted in my past life didn't matter anymore.

Before I could give my answer, the air suddenly became thick and hazy. The surrounding energy wafted back and forth. Several ghost-like women materialized out of the fog in an ephemeral circle around us. They stood silently staring at me. I looked at Von and shuddered with fear.

"Do not be afraid," he said. "These are your ancestors. They show their approval. Will you accept your role as Domina Lumen with me as your guardian?"

I looked into Von's crystalline eyes. This was it. I was standing at the crossroads. I had to make a decision. Everyone was counting on me. There really was no choice. There was only one answer.

"Yes."

Then a strong wind swept around us, gusting upwards into the night sky. Lightning struck nearby. The women vanished. The fog dissipated. The surrounding energy grew cold and sharp. Something wasn't right.

"Go inside! Now!" Von commanded, taking my hand. I hurriedly shoved Athas into my pocket as we climbed the embankment and rushed toward the house. When we arrived, Von opened the sliding glass door and gently pushed me inside.

"Lock this and don't come out until I return." He closed the door between us then leaped off the deck and disappeared into the night.

12. Đan

The sudden change in the atmosphere and Von's abrupt departure must have meant Kraegon was near. I was vulnerable without my guardian. Von had already proven energy entities could walk through doors. What would stop Kraegon from coming in? I scanned the house for a place to hide then remembered seeing a tiny cedar closet in the loft.

I ran upstairs. When I reached the last step I noticed something on the bed that hadn't been there before. The room was too dim to see what it was. I lit the candle by the bed and saw a small black, wooden box with Celtic-looking designs carved on the sides. Carved on the top was a snake coiled in a circle holding its tail in its mouth. A gold metal clasp held the lid shut. There was no lock.

I gently lifted the lid. Inside, there lay a handwritten note.

"*Ysolde,*

Nix is a Guardian of the Stone. Please give Athas to him and allow him to coil around your neck. Nix will defend the stone to his death. He is quite poisonous, but should pose no threat to you. You must trust him. — Von"

I placed the candle close to the box and looked inside, but could see nothing. I cautiously lowered a fingertip into the opening and felt something cool and scaly. It moved. I jerked my hand back and brought the candle closer to look again. A foot-long black snake slowly wound his way out of the box. His amber eyes shimmered as he flicked his tongue.

I took Athas out of my pocket and placed the stone on the bed near the box. The snake immediately slithered to the stone then wrapped his tail around it. He slid onto my hand and up my arm, dragging the stone behind. He glided across my collar bone then around the back of my neck, under my hair. My skin crawled. I held my breath. The snake circled my neck then locked his jaws around his tail.

I stood up and held the candle to a small mirror on the wall. The effect was a shimmering black choker that was alive. The snake peered at me for a moment then closed his eyes. I gently stroked his cool skin. I'd have to wear turtle necks in class from now on or become known as a total freak on campus. Who was I kidding? My days of going to school were probably numbered.

Rain began to fall against the window pane. I took the candle into the empty cedar closet, closed the door and sat on the floor. My hand caressed Athas. I gently pulled on the stone, wanting to put it back in my pocket where I knew it would be safe, but Nix held it firmly in place. I kept my hand on the stone and leaned my head against the side of the closet. Soon the candle went out. My eyelids grew heavy and I fell asleep.

The dream of the dark-haired man in the canyon returned. He was beckoning me to step off the rim, just like before, but this time I felt there was someone else in the dream.

"Ysolde, help me." I heard Dan's voice drift through the air in a loud whisper.

I turned from the edge of the canyon in my dream to look behind me. "Dan?"

"Help me." His voice faded into the mist rising from the abyss then the canyon vanished into black nothingness. I woke up in the closet and opened my eyes, but could see only darkness. I placed my hand at my neck and felt the cold body of Nix still holding Athas securely.

Dan's faint voice returned, this time from inside the house. "I'm dying, Ysolde."

"Where are you, Dan?" I scrambled out of the closet.

"Ysolde, help."

To hell with Kraegon. I fumbled for the light switch on the wall and turned it on.

"Dan!" I shouted, looking down from the loft, straining to hear a response. All remained quiet, then lightning struck and the thunder shook the house. A storm was raging outside.

I felt a cool draft and hurried downstairs. The sliding glass door leading out to the deck was open. I dashed through it into the rain. Maybe Von had returned. I couldn't see anything through the pelting sheets. I could only hear thunder and the swollen, rushing water of the river below.

"Dan! Von!" I shouted into the night. Where was Von? I needed him. Was that really Dan's voice I heard or Kraegon playing a trick to lure me out? I couldn't take a chance. If that *was* Dan, I had to rescue him with or without help.

I hurried back inside and raced upstairs, grabbing my jacket and backpack. I ran through the kitchen, opening drawers, looking for some kind of weapon to take. I found a long kitchen knife and stuffed it into the outer pocket of my backpack.

The lightning of the storm had become intense and dangerously close. Only a fool would go out, but all I could think about was finding Dan. If Kraegon had him in his world, I'd have to use the vortex which I knew practically nothing about. I had no idea what I was doing, but I knew I had to do something.

I jumped off the deck and slipped down the muddy slope to the river. A lightning bolt hit nearby, its thunder shook the ground. My body began trembling. I took deep breaths while walking around the area. Where was that energy line I found earlier? I was going too fast. I had to slow down and concentrate.

The river was flooded over the bank where the line had been. I waded through the rushing water. The strong current pushed against my legs, making it hard to keep my balance. The rain was pouring in sheets. My body was drenched. I closed my eyes. After a few baby steps, I felt a warm tingle in my left hand. When I stepped back, the feeling was gone. I stepped forward again and the tingling returned. I found it!

I stroked Nix a few times then gently pulled on the stone. He loosened his grip allowing Athas to fall into my palm. My hand was shaking so badly I feared I might drop the stone into the river. But somehow I managed to hold Athas steady long enough to allow the positive energy line to align with the stone. I turned the stone clockwise. Nothing happened. I tried again. Nothing. Maybe this wasn't the right spot.

I took careful steps around the area, feeling for another tingle. The rain was coming down so hard it felt like bullets piercing my jacket and exposed skin. I tightened my hood around my face. Dan's voice suddenly flooded the air around me.

"I'm dying, Ysolde. Please . . ."

"I'm coming, Dan!" His voice was eerie and ghostlike, fading in and out.

I cautiously waded back to the original spot and the tingling returned. I turned the stone deliberately this time, concentrating on the vision of the vortex. A strong shift in the surrounding energy made me feel light-headed. The space around me began to warp back and forth, then the vortex materialized.

I stared at the mysterious opening for a moment, having no idea what would happen when I stepped into it. How could I be sure it would go to Kraegon's world and to Dan? Maybe I'd end up somewhere else. What if I couldn't come back?

I took a step closer. The hole began to pull me toward it. I gave Athas back to Nix and grasped them both tightly then I closed my eyes and leaned forward.

My body was instantly sucked in. I rushed face first through shimmering lights at warp speed. The extreme motion pulled my hair and skin on my face back so tightly I thought they would peel off. The tunnel twisted back and forth, up and down like a runaway rollercoaster. I was so petrified I couldn't feel my heartbeat or my breath. My mind was filled with adrenaline and terror for what was to come.

After flying with great speed through the tunnel for what seemed like only a few minutes, the speed began to slow down then I came to a sudden stop and found myself floating upright in a black void. There was nothing above me or below. There were no sounds, no vibrations of energy, no wind, no sense that anything else existed – an infinite nothingness. I was in a strange deep space without any stars or planets. The only positive was somehow I could still breathe.

I checked Nix. He held Athas securely wrapped within his tail. How could I find Dan in this void? I tried to swim in the air. I couldn't make myself go forward or backward. Was I dead? Surely there was more to being dead than this for all eternity. Even if I could move, I had no idea which way to go.

"Hello?" I yelled. My muffled voice stopped short as if an invisible wall was directly in front of me.

There had to be a way to start moving again toward Dan. I thought about Oma's wise words and all the things she tried to teach me, even though I wasn't always listening. She taught me that our thoughts were things. She said we could even create our own worlds with our thoughts. It sounded ridiculous at the time, but not so much now. Maybe my thoughts could take me to Dan.

I visualized Dan standing before me. I repeated to myself, *take me to Dan, take me to Dan*. Almost immediately, my body began twisting in and out of the void. Then it broke free. I was thrust back into the tunnel of lights going warp speed again.

After a few minutes, I came to another abrupt halt. This time, instead of the black void, the tunnel was replaced with a shimmering gray fog pressing up against me as if it were alive and trying to make me move in a certain direction. Faceless creatures emerged from the fog. They were walking about, some reaching out to touch me. I recoiled from their long tentacle-like fingers. One of the creatures reached for the stone. I smacked its fingers away and dashed forward into the mist.

The surface I was running on was like an invisible waterbed. It waved up and down each time my foot stepped on it. I saw a faint glow in the distance and pushed my way through the foggy creatures toward it. The creatures faded as I passed them, morphing into what looked like dragons with huge barbed wings. The energy from their wing beats pushed me from side to side as I continued to run between them.

Take me to Dan, take me to Dan, I kept mumbling under my trembling breath. My body was tingling with cold, giving me the sense I was heading in the right direction toward Kraegon. I was still surrounded by the thick haze, but now felt a resistance, an invisible force slowing me down. The waterbed sensation turned to trudging through mud as the fog began to thicken. A putrid smell of sulfur filled the air.

Soon walking became too difficult. I fell forward, attempting to pull myself through the density on my hands and knees. I ran out of breath and stopped, still muttering my request between gasps. My eyes darted back and forth at the flying dragons circling around me.

This world was multi-leveled like layers of glass stacked one upon another. I could look up and see the glistening bellies of the dragons and look down and see their spiked backs. They seemed to be herding me in the direction of the light.

I looked over my shoulder and saw nothing but black emptiness where there used to be gray fog. The void was closing in upon me. I reached up to take Athas from Nix, afraid something would happen to him. I needed to make sure the stone was safe in my pocket. Nix wouldn't let go of the stone. The harder I pulled, the more strangling his grasp became around my neck. I could barely breathe.

"Nix! Let go!" I pleaded.

I gripped his cold, slick body with both hands and yanked as hard as I could. A sudden sharp pain pierced my hand as he sank his fangs into my skin.

"Ouch! Dammit!"

I jerked away from him and examined the two small puncture wounds, remembering Von's note. *"He's quite poisonous."*

I was trapped with Nix wrapped next to my jugular not letting me have Athas and Kraegon somewhere close by. I sucked the puncture wound, spitting out as much venom as I could and cursed Von for thinking a slithering reptile was better than I was at keeping Athas safe.

The black dragons created a swirling, invisible cage around me. I knew Kraegon was watching. He had intentionally lured me to his lair. But where was he? Where was Dan?

"Kraegon!" I yelled into the mist as I pulled the kitchen knife from my backpack. "You can have me in trade for Dan!"

I turned around, holding the knife in front of me, looking above and below for any response.

"I want Von," a low-pitched voice boomed through the fog behind me.

I turned around, but could only see the gray mass clinging to my face. Tiny sparks flickered within it.

"It's only me," I shouted. "You can have the stone if you let Dan go." Von and Oma would never forgive me, but I didn't care. Dan was more important.

I waited for the dark image of Kraegon to appear. The dragons landed one at a time, forming a circle around me. Their eyes glowed as their long spiked tails whipped around like cats watching a bird, waiting for the moment to pounce.

"I want Von," repeated the voice.

"Take *me* instead!" I cried in desperation.

Then suddenly I felt strong fingers curl around my shoulder, gripping it tightly. There was nothing behind me but fog. I jumped away in horror and began running back toward the void. I didn't know what to do. Was Dan really here? My survival instincts were telling me to run like hell.

A voice that sounded like Von shouted, "Ysolde, stop! I'm here now!"

I kept running. It couldn't be Von. He needed me to open the vortex before he could enter Kraegon's world. It must be another one of Kraegon's tricks. The void was just ahead. I would leap into it and concentrate on going home. I had fallen for Kraegon's ruse. Dan was probably safe back in Texas with Oma.

"Stop, now!" The voice commanded. "You can't go back into the void, Ysolde. You'll be ripped apart. Stop!"

"Stop, Ysolde! Please!" This time it was Dan's voice. Kraegon would never try to protect me from dying, would he? I slowed down and stopped at the edge of the void, ready to jump.

"I'm here." Someone that looked like Von suddenly emerged through the mist standing just a few yards away. "I will protect you now."

"How do I know you're really Von?"

"Because Furia would trust me." No one knew about Furia except Dan and Von. Sudden warmth coursed through my body. I looked into his crystalline blue eyes. He smiled gently.

"Von! It is you."

He pulled my tense body to him and held me closely.

"Where did you go when you jumped off the deck? I needed you," I said.

"I'm sorry. One of Kraegon's allies was near the river."

"But, how did you get here without the vortex?"

"The one you opened was still there when I returned to the house."

"I thought I heard Dan calling for help. But I think it was just Kraegon tricking me. I've been such a fool to come here and risk everything."

"No, you were right. Kraegon has Dan in a crystal."

"What? In a crystal? Is he still alive?"

"He is for now, but there's no time to waste."

"How will we get him back?"

"There is only one way for the both of you to leave here safely."

"You!" Kraegon's voice echoed through the fog. I jumped with fright. Von pulled me behind him. "At last, you have come to my house, Von. Welcome!"

Kraegon materialized from the mist. His long black hair flowed loosely around his handsome face. His steel blue eyes laughed with delight. It was the man from my canyon dreams. He gazed at the two of us for a moment.

"How touching. What a blissfully dysfunctional couple you could make if you were alive, but alas," he jeered, walking closer.

Von stepped toward him.

"Kraegon. It's been a while since I've seen you face-to-face. I'm usually staring at your ass running away," he taunted.

Kraegon's eyes lit up. "Yes, you're good at following the leader. I see this time you followed your heart. Pity to be so sentimental. So uncharacteristic of such a great warrior as yourself," he sniffed with sarcasm. "And Ysolde, remember your parents? Let's just say I enjoyed them immensely."

"You bastard!" I leaped toward him. Von's grip pulled me back.

"She's a lively one. Just like the original Ysolde. I remember how fond you were of her. I will enjoy taking my time with this one."

"You can't have her," Von stated firmly.

"Yes, I believe I can. You're in *my* world now." Kraegon walked calmly around us, his arms clasped behind his back, eyeing Athas as he passed. Von turned to face him as he came close.

"You can have me *and* the stone, if you'll let Ysolde and her brother go."

"An interesting proposition, but as you know, she must be dead for the stone to work for me so why would I let her go?" Kraegon leaned toward me and closed his eyes, inhaling deeply. His nostrils flared. "She has such a sweet aura of energy."

"Leave her alone," Von warned.

"I do what I want in my world. What's stopping me from disintegrating you, taking Ysolde and the stone *and* having her brother as a snack?" he chuckled.

"My friends have captured something precious to you," said Von.

"What could you possibly have that would interest me?"

"Kikka, your sister."

"Kikka? She's annihilating Lumen for me on the world within."

"Not anymore. She was recently caught during a lightning storm. We will trade her for the safety of Ysolde and her brother."

"Show me proof that you have her."

Von held his palm toward Kraegon. A small orb began to glow a radiant rose color, then a pattern of lights repeatedly flashed within the glow.

Kraegon drew in a sudden breath. His eyes widened with shock.

"Kikka's energy signature," Von stated confidently. "Take me and the stone, let Ysolde and her brother go and I will give your sister to you."

I whispered to Von, "I'm not leaving unless the three of us go together."

Von turned and looked into my eyes, "Trust me." He looked back at Kraegon. "Do we have a deal?"

"No. The stone is of no use to me as long as Ysolde is alive."

"After you've killed me, Ysolde will be easy prey," Von pointed out.

I stared at Von with complete astonishment. He avoided my gaze. What he was saying was true. If he stayed and I returned without him, I would be dead before the day was out. He clearly had a plan in mind, but I didn't like it.

I stepped in front of Von and looked Kraegon directly in the eye. "Let my brother and Von go. You can have me. I'm all you really want."

"That's not an option," Von interrupted, pushing me back behind him. "If you want Kikka to survive, you'll take me and the stone."

"Your bickering amuses me," Kraegon laughed. "I do care about Kikka, even though she rarely cares about me. And you're right. Ysolde will be pathetically easy to kill once you're gone. No game at all, really. Once she's dead and you're out of the way, I will have full control of all the energy lines. My armies will take over the world within and swarm the energy fields of Earth. I will be unstoppable. Yes, we have a deal."

"Give me her brother then you can have the stone," Von said.

"And you," added Kraegon.

"Yes."

Kraegon snapped his fingers. A small red dragon flew over beside him, lowering its head. Kraegon pulled a chain from the dragon's neck that held a clear crystal pendant. The crystal glowed a brilliant blue.

"Your brother is in this crystal. I find it's much easier to store humans this way. You better hurry, though. His time is running out."

Von turned to me and said quietly, "Let me have Athas. I promise you will get him back."

"I'm supposed to guard the stone with my life," I whispered back. "I won't let you do this. I won't leave you here to die."

"You will see me and Athas again. If you want to rescue your brother, you must give me the stone."

"Nix won't let me. He bit me last time I tried."

"He'll let you this time. Try again."

I nervously touched Nix. He remained still. I gently wrapped my fingers around the stone. He released his grip, letting it fall into my hand. I was betraying Oma and all my ancestors. I was betraying the world, allowing Kraegon to have the stone. Once I was dead, he would have complete power over the positive and negative energy lines. How could Von get the stone back? How could he come back without the vortex? He would be stuck in the negative energy world forever.

Von reached out to touch my hand. His heat radiated throughout my body. My muscles tensed as I let go of the stone.

"Thank you. You did the right thing," he said. I couldn't look at him. I diverted my gaze in anguish and shame.

"Give it to me," demanded Kraegon.

"You must give me the crystal first," Von commanded.

"Here, catch!" Kraegon tossed the crystal into the fog.

"Dan!" I yelled as I leapt into the air with my arms outstretched to catch it, but the crystal vanished into the haze. "No!" I screamed.

Von disappeared then reappeared in seconds. He grabbed my hand. "Put this in a safe place," he said as he handed Dan's crystal to me.

I held the crystal in my palm. It was warm and glowed brightly with tiny flickering lights.

"How do I get him out of there?"

"When you return, my sister Amara and a Lumen wolf named Kolt will meet you. They will release him from the crystal. You must go now. The longer Dan stays in the crystal, the harder it will be to remove him. The stone is absorbing his energy."

I pushed the crystal into my jeans pocket then gazed into Von's eyes one last time. He wiped a tear from my cheek. I buried my face in his hand. "Trust me," he whispered again.

"I do trust you, but how will you get back?"

"Amara and Kolt know the plan. They'll help you, Ysolde. Let them become part of your family. Now go, before it's too late."

Von slowly drew his hand away and walked toward Kraegon. I watched helplessly as his tall, graceful form disappeared into the smoky vapor.

"My pets will escort you back to your homeland, Ysolde," Kraegon shouted from somewhere within the gray haze. "Don't be afraid," he said, laughing out loud. "See you soon."

Before I could react, I was swept onto the back of a blue-violet dragon. Its shimmery scales reminded me of Nix's slick skin. I leaned down with both hands firmly grasping the great beast's neck as we soared through the fog, toward the black void.

13. AMARA & KOLT

When we reached the void, I was thrust back into the tunnel of lights, racing through space. Within what seemed like a few seconds, I was suddenly back in Abysmal, standing next to the river at night.

I felt Dan's crystal still in my pocket and breathed a sigh of relief. I touched my neck, checking for Nix, but he was gone. He was probably with Von, now that I no longer had the stone. The puncture wounds on my hand from his bite had disappeared, as if they never had existed. I understood why Nix bit me. He was protecting Athas, just as I was trying to. And I failed. All my faith was now in Von to somehow return safely with the stone.

I climbed up the muddy embankment to Cam's house. The rain was still pouring. I wondered if any real time had passed at all. Von had said Amara and Kolt would be waiting for me.

The house was warm, dry and empty. Soaked through, exhausted and hungry, I went upstairs and changed into dry clothes. I took Dan's crystal out of my dirty jean's pocket and inspected it closely, wondering if he could see or hear anything. The crystal's blue light was fading. We had to get him out before it was too late.

I hurried downstairs, made a quick bowl of soup and ate it while sitting on the couch, watching for Amara and Kolt. Dan's crystal lay by my side. Lightning feathered across the sky followed by the rumblings of rolling thunder. Was that real lightning or Kraegon? I shuddered at the thought, feeling isolated and alone.

My cell phone began ringing upstairs. I ran to the loft and grabbed it just as the call went to voicemail.

"Dammit!" I pushed the button to hear the message.

"Ysolde, this is Cam. I'll be there around noon tomorrow. Hope everything's okay."

If you only knew. Part of me was still in Kraegon's world with Von. The other part was here, wondering if my brother was going to die stuck inside a crystal. And Cam was coming home. His life would be in danger if I stayed in his house, but I had nowhere else to go. It was just as well I missed his call. I wouldn't know what to say to him.

Dan's blue light was barely visible now. He couldn't wait any longer. Where were Amara and Kolt? If they weren't coming to me, I'd have to go out and find them. I rushed back downstairs and pushed Dan's crystal deep inside my pocket. As I was heading out the sliding glass door, a huge bolt of lightning flashed. In that brief moment of light, I saw a girl and a white wolf down by the river bounding toward the house. I instantly recognized them from the night I drove on the highway and when I saw them in the woods behind the art building. Amara and Kolt!

"Amara!" I yelled as I stepped out the door and waved in her direction. Dan would be okay now. A new sense of hope filled my heart. I slid down the embankment to meet them.

As soon as they crossed the river I thrust my hand toward Amara. "Welcome! I'm Ysolde!"

She remained quiet and kept her hand by her side. Her look was calm and expressionless as she gazed into my eyes, studying my face. She didn't seem to be out of breath at all after her sprint. Her long white, blonde hair hung loosely, framing her pale, delicate features. Her petite body was clothed in jeans, boots and a jacket similar to mine. She had the same brilliant blue eyes of Von.

"I am so glad to see both of you! I've been waiting and wondering and now you're finally here!" I said, feeling overly excited at this point, but I couldn't help it. Amara continued to stare at me in silence then she finally spoke.

"This is Kolt." She looked down at the handsome white wolf. Her voice was clear and precise.

I reached out to pet him. Kolt looked at me with black-lined, gray eyes and raised his front lip, showing his razor-sharp fangs. I slowly pulled my hand back.

"I've seen you and Von and Kolt running in the woods."

"We work as a team. Von is my brother," said Amara. "Kolt is our tracker."

I pulled the crystal from my pocket and handed it to her. "Dan's light is fading. Is he dying?"

She held the crystal up and gazed into it. "He's becoming part of the crystal. We need to extract him tonight."

Kolt nudged Amara softly. "Kolt says there are no Vapors in the area. It's time to go to our underground lair to help your brother." She and Kolt turned toward the river and started to leave.

"Wait!" I said. "I should leave a note for my friend Cam in case I'm not here when he gets back tomorrow."

I scrambled up the muddy ledge and ran into the house then scribbled a short message on a paper towel.

"Cam, I've gone to school. Not sure when I'll be back. – Ysolde."

I hated lying to him, but I couldn't possibly tell him that I'd gone with two energy entities to their underground lair to release Dan from a crystal. Who would believe that?

I locked the door, making sure to put the key under the stone pig and hurried back to the river.

"I'm ready," I said to Amara.

"Follow us closely."

"We could take my Jeep if it would be faster," I offered.

"Your Jeep can't go where we're headed and even if it could, we don't want to draw attention to ourselves. Let's go."

We trekked away from town, deep into the forest. The rain storm had passed. Moonlight helped me see, but fallen tree branches hidden in the shadows made it difficult to keep up. Amara and Kolt leaped over them effortlessly.

"How much farther?" I said loudly from the back of the pack. My chest was heaving for air. Amara turned in my direction with a scowl on her face.

"Don't yell unless you want Vapors swarming on top of us," she scolded. "We're almost there. Why are humans so loud and insensitive? Try to be quiet, if that's possible."

"Sorry," I whispered.

I was sensing Amara and Von were very different even if they were siblings. It was obvious I was a nuisance to her. The fact that I was the Domina Lumen apparently meant nothing. Granted, I didn't look the part. I'm sure she treated Oma with respect and it was clear that I wasn't Oma.

We walked another thirty minutes at least then came into an area near the foot of a mountain with large boulders lying at the base.

"We're here," she said.

I stopped and leaned against a tree to catch my breath. Nothing looked like a lair. "I don't see anything."

"It's underground, directly beneath your feet. Can't you feel the energy coming up?"

I stood still, waiting to feel the tingling sensations, but felt nothing. I had a feeling this was the first of many tests Amara would be putting me through. I closed my eyes and tried to concentrate. Rivers of energy suddenly shot up through my legs.

"Now I feel it."

141

"This is where we go down to our home here in your world. It's a strong positive energy line. We enter it in our energy forms."

"How do I get down there?"

"You'll have to go through that old mine shaft." Amara pointed toward the mountain about fifty yards away. I strained to see the shaft in the moonlight. The mountain had a hole in its side with debris covering part of the entrance. From a distance, the hole looked barely big enough to squeeze through.

"Once you enter the shaft, you'll crawl through it until you reach a cave. I'll meet you at that point," she said.

"Crawl through *that* hole? It doesn't look big enough. Isn't there some other way?" I had inherited a touch of claustrophobia from Mom and it was screaming inside me not to go. My heart began to race. My palms felt sweaty.

"Kolt will go with you." She looked down at the wolf. He glared back then walked away, growling softly. Amara knelt beside him. She gently stroked his face then whispered something in his ear. He looked at me, shook his fur then trotted toward the hole.

"I'll see you two soon." She suddenly vanished, leaving a flurry of sparks behind.

The white wolf stood at the mouth of the mine, barking urgently in my direction.

"Okay, okay, I'm coming. I hate small, dark, creepy, cramped spaces that could bury me alive," I muttered under my breath as I walked toward the death trap.

When I reached the opening, I saw that it was even smaller than I thought – maybe three feet in diameter. A feeling of suffocation came over me before I even went in.

Kolt jumped inside, barking all the while. I leaned forward and peeked into the pitch black interior. My hands pulled some of the rocks and debris away to make the entrance a little wider. Kolt suddenly stuck his nose out of the hole into my face. I jumped back.

"Dammit! Don't do that!" He leaped out and ran around me barking a few times then leaped back in. "Okay, I get it. You want me to go in. Just give me a minute."

I gulped clean mountain air into my lungs, looked up at the moon one last time then bent over and began crawling on my hands and knees through the mine shaft entrance.

The tunnel smelled of damp dirt and stale air. There were shards of sharp rock underneath my knees and hands. I winced as I crawled, wishing I'd worn gloves. I pulled the ends of my jacket sleeves under my palms. The mine shaft was completely dark, like the black void I'd experienced in Kraegon's world.

Soon, the shaft began to narrow. My head was dragging on the top, causing dirt to continually fall into my hair and face. I had to keep my mouth wide open to breathe the thin air. Dirt began accumulating around my lips. I could feel myself starting to panic. What if I got stuck and couldn't move?

"Where are you?" I yelled weakly through the stagnant air. Kolt barked a few times from the blackness up ahead. I wanted to go back, but how would I do that? I would have to back out. That wasn't an option. I forced myself to crawl faster.

About twenty feet more, I felt a little bit of air moving through the shaft. My neck ached from holding it up in an awkward position for so long. I stopped to rest for a minute, laying my head on my hands. More cool air came through the shaft. It gave me hope. Kolt started barking repeatedly. I followed his voice, dragging my body through the tunnel until I saw a faint light up ahead.

I heard Amara shout into the tunnel. "You're almost to the cave."

"Yeah, okay," I muttered, spitting out bits of earth. I gripped the dirt with my fingernails and pulled as hard as I could while pushing with the toes of my boots, struggling to pull my body through the narrowest part of the shaft.

At last I came to the exit. Through the opening I could see Kolt already in the cave. Amara was standing next to him, holding a tall white candle illuminating the area. She reached up and grabbed my hand then pulled me out face first. I fell onto the damp floor, my muscles weak and trembling. Kolt licked the dirt off my face and nuzzled me for a moment.

"There's no time to waste," Amara said as she helped me stand up. I shook the dirt clods from my hair and tried to wipe the dust out of my eyes.

"Not too far to go now. Follow me." She turned and briskly walked away taking the light with her. Kolt trotted close behind. I trudged after them trying to keep up.

The cave was cool, moist and quiet. I had no idea how big it was, but it was large enough for us to stand upright with ease. We walked a short distance then came to a fork where the cave divided in two. I followed the light as Amara turned to the right. Just a little farther on we came to a huge, beautifully carved wooden door. It reminded me of the carved door to Oma's house.

"A door inside a cave?" I said.

Amara lifted the golden latch, opening the door slightly then turned toward me, her face glowing.

"Welcome." She smiled softly for the first time since we had met.

We stepped inside a rounded stone area the size of a small house. Amara lit several candles, placing the largest one in an ornate metal holder near the door. The murky interior gave way to a soft radiance that increased in intensity as each candle was lit.

As the light increased, I could see stone walls inlaid with hundreds of clear quartz crystals. Pointed tips jutted out at odd angles, sparkling like diamonds. The floor was made of smooth inlaid gray stones. In the middle of the room was a gleaming black boulder about waist high. A huge multi-faceted quartz crystal lay upon it.

"Thirsty?" She handed me a crystal goblet filled with water.

I gently grasped the sparkling chalice from her hand and told her thanks, then gulped the water down, washing away the dust in my throat. Amara's demeanor had changed. She was friendly and warm, maybe because she was in her Earth home. I began to feel more at ease around her.

"So this is your lair?" I glanced around, admiring the beautiful gems and stones.

"When we're in human form on Earth, we must have a safe place to regenerate our energy."

"How do you regenerate?"

She walked over to the large crystal on the boulder and stroked it lightly with her index finger. "We absorb a crystal's energy into our energy field, making certain not to deplete it so it can regenerate and become whole again. We respect that crystals are living energy entities just as we are."

I gently touched the crystal around my neck and thought about how much my life had changed in the past month.

"Will you need to return to your energy form to get Dan out of the crystal?"

"Yes. Are you ready?"

"I'm ready." I pulled Dan's crystal out of my pocket. The gem had darkened. There were only a few tiny flecks of light twinkling inside the cloudy mass. My heart sank.

"Oh no! We're too late!" I cried as I handed it to Amara.

"We must hurry. Stand over by the door, Ysolde. Do not come any closer, no matter what you see or hear."

I leaned against the door. Kolt stood next to Amara. She placed Dan's crystal on top of the large crystal in the center of the room, then stepped back and closed her eyes. In the next few minutes, the stone walls of the room began to warp back and forth. Each time the walls wavered, my breath was taken away. My vision blurred and Amara and Kolt began to fade until they were nearly transparent then their human forms were replaced by two floating, glowing spheres.

The spheres revolved around the large crystal then both merged into one, engulfing Dan's crystal. A blinding white mass filled the middle of the room. I squinted, trying to keep my eyes open. My skin was warm and flushed. Static electricity suddenly filled the air. I could feel wisps of my hair being pulled toward the ceiling.

Then I heard a loud crack like a wooden baseball. A cumulous-type cloud formed, hovering above the crystal. Lightning bolts darted wildly around the room. I cringed on the floor, covering my head with my arms. Then everything went black.

I found myself drifting in a void again. My dizziness went away. There were no feelings of anxiety or worry, just perfect tranquility.

"Ysolde! Are you okay? Wake up!" Someone was grabbing my arms, shaking me.

"Ysolde!" I felt a severe slap to my face.

"Ouch!" I opened my eyes, feeling the hot sting on my cheek. My vision was still blurry. I tried to focus.

"You scared the hell out of me!" I realized it was Dan speaking. He clamped his hands around my arms and lifted me up against the door. I was immediately taken back to the moment he rescued me from the canyon rim.

"Dan! You're alive!" I threw my arms around him.

"Can't – breathe," he chuckled.

Amara and Kolt were back in human form. She was standing behind Dan staring at me with a worried look on her face.

"What happened?" I asked.

"I had forgotten how intense it can be for a human to be nearby when we transfer energy. You were struck by an energy bolt," Amara said.

Kolt trotted over next to me and licked my hand. I cautiously stroked his fur. He raised his lip, showing a fang, but this time I believed it meant he was happy.

"All that really matters is that Dan is back." I smiled at him. "I have so much to tell you. You're not going to believe it."

"I've got about a thousand questions for you, sis." I noticed he was rubbing the back of his neck.

"You feel okay?" I asked.

"Considering I've been stuck in a crystal? I'd say I'm doing great! I'm hungry as hell."

"I bet," I laughed.

"I don't know where we are right now, but we need to get to Cam's house where you'll be safe," he said. His face became serious. He didn't realize how safe this cave was compared to anywhere else in Abysmal.

I asked Amara what we could do about Von. She said she'd know something by this evening and for me not to leave Cam's tonight.

"I don't know how Cam will take all this. Guess we'll have to tell him now," I said.

"That would be a good idea," she said. "Cam's in danger as long as you are staying with him."

No one was safe around me. I was a walking target as long as Kraegon was alive. Was this how my life was going to be from now on?

"We'll lead you two back to the tunnel. Let's go." Amara picked up the tall white candle and led us into the cave.

"Wow," Dan said.

The candlelight faded as Amara hurried around the corner.

"Go!" I said, shoving him gently to make him move a little faster. "I don't know my way and we don't have a light."

"This cave is cool! I'm coming back to explore it sometime," he said.

"Be my guest, just not with me."

We bumped our way through the dimly lit stone walls and made it to the tunnel entrance. Kolt wagged his tail looking up at me.

"Are you going with me again, Kolt?"

He shook his fur and walked over next to Amara.

"I'll take that as a no," I said, a little disappointed.

"You'll be okay," Amara said. "There's only one way out. Just don't stop."

"Thanks, again." I said. Amara nodded.

"We'll be watching you on your way back. Remember, Kraegon could be out there, anywhere."

"Who's Kraegon?" Dan asked.

"I'll tell you on the hike back." I pulled my sleeves over my hands to protect them. "By the way, the tunnel is a tight squeeze. Don't be afraid," I teased as I climbed into the narrow shaft, pretending like it wasn't going to bother me. My heart was already racing and palms sweating from the thought of squeezing back through.

"Me? Afraid? This is great!" he said, crawling into the hole behind me.

"Yeah, it's *awesome*." I was spitting dirt out of my mouth already.

I crawled through the tunnel as fast as I could with Dan close behind. I kept my head down next to the ground and my eyes closed.

"Hey, keep your boots out of my face!" Dan shouted.

"Back off a little and that won't be a problem!" I yelled between gasps for air.

"Or *you* could speed up!"

We had been back together for less than an hour and we were already bickering. I loved it.

14. RETURN

Dan and I finally made it to the end of the tunnel. I pulled myself out into the fresh air and shook the dirt from my clothes. Dan came out soon after. He didn't seem to mind the dirt and grime that had adhered to his face and clothes. I reached up and flicked some clods out of his shaggy, blonde hair.

"Hey!" He pushed my hand away.

"Let's go, handsome."

We hiked back toward Cam's house just as dawn was breaking over the mountains. The sky was changing from blue violet to lavender. The hike was still strenuous, but being able to see where we were going made it a little easier.

As we made our way through the woods, I told Dan that I was known as the Domina Lumen now. I told him about Von, Amara and Kolt being energy entities called Lumen and about Kraegon, who was a Vapor. He learned about Nix and Athas and how important it was that Von gets the stone back from Kraegon. Then I told him I had learned Kraegon was responsible for our parent's deaths. Dan became enraged and vowed to be the one to kill Kraegon himself. It took me a while to convince him that he alone couldn't kill such a powerful entity. We had to depend on Von and the other Lumen to help. Finally, there was the bad news about my roommate Tiff and the other students who had died in the canyon. It was an information overload, but he had to be told.

"What happened back in Texas before you were put in the crystal?" I asked. "Did you see anything or anyone who might have been Kraegon?"

"All I remember is being outside tending to Oma's garden then everything went black."

"You don't remember being put in the crystal?"

"Not at all. It's like I was unconscious the whole time I was in that rock. I'm worried about Oma. She's alone with no one to protect her."

"The Lumen are supposed to be watching out for her. We can ask Amara."

When we made it to the river near Cam's house, I saw his truck in the driveway.

"Dammit, he's home. He wasn't supposed to be here until afternoon. What are we going to tell him?"

"I'll tell him I came for a surprise visit and we've been hiking. We can tell him the rest later," Dan said.

"You think he'll believe all this?"

"Cam's into some pretty weird stuff with his archaeology, though he may wonder what we've been smoking." The corners of Dan's lips rose.

"Not funny," I said.

"Yes it is. You're too serious."

"My job as Domina Lumen *is* serious. I'm finding out just *how* serious it is and it scares me to death."

"Oh, you mean because you're expected to banish Kraegon and save the world? You do realize how crazy all of this sounds, don't you?"

"Yeah, believe me, I do. But you must believe it now, since you were actually squished down inside a crystal."

"Wish I had a picture of that. What a cool selfie!"

"Oh my God, do you ever take anything seriously?"

"Yes, like I can't believe Oma gave this Domina Lumina job to you."

"Lumen."

"Whatever. Why not me? I'm the brave, adventurous one."

"Really? Furia's pretty damn brave."

"Excuse me. You're not playing the game right now. Furia's just a bunch of pixels."

"You're not a dowser."

"Is that all it takes? I can swing a rock around on a chain."

I laughed. "Okay, but you're not a girl. That's the other requirement."

"Well, excuse *me*."

"Enough goofing around. Let's go see Cam."

"Yes, your high ass." Dan bowed deeply.

We crossed the river then hiked up the embankment. I opened the sliding glass door. Cam was cooking something on the stove. He turned when he heard my voice and saw Dan walking in.

"Dan? Hey bud!" he said with a big smile, his soft green eyes twinkling. "What a surprise! When did you get here?" He hurried over to Dan and gave him a big hug.

Dan's face lit up when he saw his best friend.

"I flew in yesterday and Ysolde picked me up. It's great to be here."

"Wow. I can't believe this! Why didn't you tell me he was coming, Ysolde?"

"I wanted it to be a surprise. That's why my note said I was at school." That excuse worked out conveniently.

Cam stood staring at us for a few minutes, both looking dirty and disheveled. He shook his head and grinned ear to ear. "Well, your plan worked. This is just like old times. Are ya'll hungry?"

"Starving!" Dan chuckled. "How've you been?"

"Busy, but good." He turned back toward the stove to mind the frying pan. "I'm making one of my famous veggie omelets."

"Just the way I like it," I said.

He looked back at me. His cheeks dimpled like a cute little kid.

"Looks like you guys went for a hike," he said.

"We hiked across the river toward the mountain," I said.

"Man, it's nice out here," Dan said, "I'm so jealous."

Cam laughed. "It's paradise, no doubt about it." He flipped the fat omelet oozing with cheese. "How long are you staying, Dan?"

"Not sure. I haven't been able to find a job since I moved back home with Oma. It seemed like a good time to come for a visit and check on little sis." Dan's lie was convincing.

"I'm glad you're here. Ysolde's been going through a rough patch. A lot of weird things have been going on around campus."

"So I hear." Dan walked over to the window. "Guess they haven't found the killer of those girls yet. I'm glad she's here with you for a few days."

"Me too. Although, I don't know how much protection I can offer when I'm not around. Still, at least she's off campus now." He reached into the cupboard for some plates.

What did he mean by saying I was "off campus *now*"? Did "now" mean living with him or just staying this weekend?

Dan raised an eyebrow at me. "Are you moving in with Cam or just spending the weekend?"

My eyes darted from Dan to Cam. I shrugged my shoulders, waiting for a reply. Cam turned around to face me, plate in hand. "Well, *are* you moving in?"

"I guess so?" I looked at Dan for approval.

"It's cool with me, considering the circumstances, as long as you have your own room and you behave yourself." He crossed his arms and gave me the big warning look he had learned from Dad.

"I will if you will, since we both know you rarely behave."

"I mean it, Ysolde. You know what I'm talking about."

"Don't worry. I have my own room. It's up there." I pointed toward the loft.

"Up there? Where the hell are the walls? All I see is a blanket hanging from the ceiling."

"She needed a place in a hurry. That's all I had to spare. She'll be okay," Cam said.

Dan walked up the steps to the loft then came back down.

"You expect her to pay rent for *that*?"

"Of course not. Ysolde is family." Cam smiled at me. "She can help with the cooking and cleaning. I could definitely use a woman's touch around here."

"Cooking and cleaning? I don't think there's any threat of that happening," Dan snickered.

"Hey, I used to help Mom clean the house and cook sometimes."

"Your idea of cooking requires a microwave."

"I learned from the best," I said, bowing to Dan.

"So you'll be an asset after all?" Cam winked at me.

"Everybody takes care of their own mess, how does that sound?" I said.

"That's fine. You know I was just teasing."

"I know."

I suddenly felt very tired and anxious. How could I joke and carry on with these guys while Von was in Kraegon's evil lair, maybe being tortured or dead? I was the Domina Lumen. I was supposed to protect Athas. Wasn't I supposed to be able to *do* something more than be some helpless human? My worlds had reversed. Hanging out with Cam and Dan used to be my reality. Now it was more like make believe. The world of the Lumen and Vapors was my reality now.

"I'm going to take a quick shower before I eat," I said.

"Good, you stink," Dan teased.

"Speak for yourself."

"Just like old times, eh?" Cam grinned at us.

I shook my head and walked upstairs to grab some clean clothes then came back down to the bathroom.

After my shower, I dressed in the bathroom then opened the window to let the steam drift out into the cool mountain air. The smell of pines filled the room. I closed my eyes and for just a moment, I was happily hiking back in the mountains as a child with my family with no worries or fears.

I heard a gentle knock and opened my eyes. Reality rushed back in. I closed the window and locked it.

"Your omelet is ready," Cam said quietly through the bathroom door. I cracked the door open. Our faces met within inches. His eyes skimmed my damp lips and hair. "You look nice." I could feel my cheeks blush with heat.

"Thanks," I said, softly brushing against him as I passed through the doorway. My attraction to Cam had not faded, but my heart was becoming etched with Von. He and I had an unearthly bond that went back centuries. I could feel his arms pulling me up from the canyon, his ice-blue eyes fixed on mine.

I sat on the couch to eat my omelet. It was made just the way I liked with mushrooms, bell peppers, black olives and mozzarella cheese. I could smell the warm olive oil. The last time I had eaten home cooked food was with Oma. She seemed near me now. I took a bite.

My mouth was filled with happiness, but my nerves were on edge. I knew I wouldn't be able to sit around and wait for news about Von from Amara. I ate half of the omelet and gave the rest to Dan.

"What's wrong? Don't you like it?" Cam asked.

"It's great. I'm just not as hungry as I thought I was. Guess I'm excited about Dan being here and moving in. If it's okay, I think I'll leave you two alone while I go get some things from my dorm room."

"If you wait a little bit, we can go with you," Cam offered.

"Thanks, but I'm not going to get that much stuff and besides, I have a few things to do on campus. You guys stay here and have fun. I shouldn't be too long."

"Okay, suit yourself." Cam flipped another omelet in the pan.

"Be careful. Don't stay gone too long." Dan's eyes told me to watch out for Kraegon and don't do anything stupid.

Doing stupid things and lying were becoming second nature to me. "See ya'll in a bit." I gathered my keys to the Jeep and walked out the door.

I drove up the road in the direction of the forest, parked the Jeep just off the road near the river then started hiking toward the mountain.

Finding the trail was harder than I thought it would be. If I'd started walking from Cam's, like I did the first time with Amara and Kolt, it would've been easier. I put my hand in my pocket to feel for the stone out of habit. Its absence gave me an empty feeling. As long as I was alive, Kraegon couldn't use Athas. He said he would be coming for me soon. I had to hurry.

I removed my pendant and dowsed for the direction of the shaft. The crystal swung around in a gentle circle a few times then began swinging strongly to the left and right. I asked if going to the right was the correct direction and the answer was yes. I headed that way.

The mountain was getting closer. I picked up the pace, sensing a slight tingling in my hands and feet. Things were beginning to feel right. I ran into a clearing that looked vaguely familiar. Was this where Amara and Kolt went into the ground in their energy forms? I suddenly felt energy streaming up from the ground. Yes, this was the spot. I strained to see up ahead. There, at the base of the mountain, was the mine shaft.

15. Deception

I ran as fast as I could and leaped into the hole head first. There was no hesitation this time. It was pitch black inside, but I knew to keep crawling until I felt the air draft coming from the cave.

As I pulled my way through the shaft, I knew for a fact that I had become a crazy person. I didn't live in the real world anymore. I was possessed with a new energy that was either going to be a good thing or my death. Worrying about my safety was at the bottom of my list until I knew Von was okay.

When a cool current of air touched my hands outstretched in front of me, I knew I was getting close to the exit. I pulled myself faster through the tunnel. As I approached the cave opening, there was no light like there had been when Amara was waiting with a candle. I'd forgotten about that part. Could I remember how to get to her door in the pitch black?

I crawled out of the hole, falling on my face on the cave floor. I wiped my face with my sleeve then started walking to the left with one hand on the rough wall.

"Amara!" I yelled. "It's Ysolde!"

The wall of the cave was cold and wet as my fingertips gently dragged along its craggy surface. I knew there would be a fork in the cave and I would go to the right, but being in the dark made judging the distance almost impossible. I stumbled to the other side of the cave and placed my right hand on the wall as a guide.

"Amara! Please help me!" I shouted again into the stifling silence, pausing to use my other senses. The black void was disorienting. I placed my left hand out in front and continued on. Then suddenly I felt a presence and stopped. Something had entered my personal space. Its aura pushed against me from behind like a thick fog. A soft breath blew on the back of my neck.

"Back so soon?" said a female voice.

"Amara! You scared the hell out of me!" My heart was hammering through my chest as I tried to catch my breath.

"You shouldn't rely so much on sight. There's so much more you could be feeling if you would just practice," she sighed. "Let me see your crystal, Ysolde. Hurry up."

I was intruding in Amara's world without an invitation this time and could sense she wasn't pleased. As I removed my pendant, Amara gently pulled the crystal from my grasp. A few seconds later, a soft blue glow illuminated our faces. She looked at the crystal as if she were communicating with it. The crystal seemed to respond with soft pulses of varying lights.

"Are you talking to it?" I asked in wonderment.

"In a way. I'm sending energy to her and she's thanking me. She had become quite depleted. A little sun or moon bathing is a good thing for a crystal now and then. You should remember that."

"My crystal is a *she*?"

"She gives off feminine energy. She is completely devoted to you."

"I had no idea." I stared quietly at the glowing, crystalline gem.

"It was foolish and dangerous for you to come alone. I was watching as you stumbled around in the dark."

"Why didn't you help me?"

"You needed to use your body dowsing skills. If you're going to strike out on your own, you can't always assume the Lumen will be there for you."

"I came about Von. Have you heard? Is he okay?"

Her eyes lowered. "Follow me," she said as she walked ahead.

Amara's face was hard to read, but I knew if Von was okay he would've been the one to greet me. I swallowed hard, holding the tears back as we wove our way to the Lumen's lair.

When we arrived, Amara opened the wooden door and Kolt came bounding up to me with a big grin. I knelt beside him and rubbed his thick fur. He licked my face repeatedly with slobbery wolf kisses. He reminded me of my German Shepherd I had as a child and the many nights he slept with me as my guardian.

"That's enough, you two," Amara groaned, shaking her head as she handed my crystal back to me. "There's someone you need to meet."

I stepped further into the dim, candlelit room. A shadowed figure crouched in the opposite corner. Amara walked over to the man and whispered something to him. The man grunted a few times. Amara gestured for me to come.

"Ysolde, this is Gutar."

The crouching figure stood and turned to face me, without acknowledging my name. He was tall and formidable in stature. He wore a thick, brown robe draped around his strong body. His face was older, with long blonde hair mixed with gray and a short, scruffy beard. His eyes were a chilling, light gray.

Gutar quietly stared at me. The shadows from the candles made his face look violent and mysterious. There was a long, awkward silence. Finally, I nervously offered, "Hello," with a slight smile and little eye contact. Gutar didn't respond.

"Gutar is our elder. The Lumen call on him when we need help," Amara said.

He breathed a heavy sigh then finally spoke. "You are the new Domina Lumen?" His tone of voice was low and measured as his eyes evaluated me.

"Yes," I said tentatively.

"You deserve to die." The huge man's face was stern. His posture became aggressive. He took a step toward me.

I backed away toward the door. Von wasn't here to protect me. My eyes darted to Amara. The corners of her mouth rose slightly in a self-satisfied grin. *What the hell?* Did she agree with him?

"It is because of your recklessness that Von is near death," he stated bluntly.

"Near death?" Von was hurt. Courage flooded my veins. "Where is he?"

"He is weak. Kraegon took his energy signature," Amara said. "Without it, he cannot go into his energy form and feed. Kolt found him outside the cave after you and Dan left."

"He's *here?*"

"Yes." There was a hint of warning in her voice. She pointed to the floor behind Gutar. I hurried over to him.

"Be easy, Ysolde," Amara instructed.

"Von! You're here and you're alive!"

I leaned down and kissed his cheek. His eyes were dull and cloudy. He looked into my eyes. A soft smile came upon his lips.

"Ysolde," he whispered breathlessly. "I must tell you something."

"Don't talk. You're too weak," said Amara. She knelt down beside him.

"Amara, you need to hear this, too. Alia has the stone." Von leaned his head back and closed his eyes to regain his strength.

"What?" I cried in shock. "How could that be? Alia? Are you sure?"

Von spoke without opening his eyes. "She is working with Kraegon. She has been all along. I can't believe I wasn't aware."

"But Alia is *human*, isn't she?" I asked.

"Yes. Kraegon is using her so she can carry the stone."

"She pretended to be your friend," Amara said.

"Did she kill Tiff?"

"Kraegon killed her, but Alia helped make it happen," Von murmured.

"So she and Kraegon were trying to kill me that day when we hiked together? No wonder she acted so strange when I let her touch the stone. She didn't want to give it back."

Amara's face became enraged. "You let her touch the stone?"

"I know. It was stupid and irresponsible." I looked down at the ground, avoiding her stare. I had already failed as the Domina Lumen in everyone's eyes.

"What about her friends? Are they like her?" I kept my eyes cast down.

"Jon, Jesse and Mags are Vapors," Von said.

How could I have been so deceived? How could I not have felt their negative energy? I recalled feeling a slight twinge when I met them, but I didn't really suspect a thing.

"I can't believe it."

"Believe it, Ysolde. Your brother, Oma and the Lumen are your only friends now," Amara said.

"What about Cam? He's not one of them, is he?"

"Not yet," Von whispered. "But Kraegon can be very persuasive."

"Cam would never turn on me."

"He wouldn't have a choice," said Amara.

Gutar stood behind me. His body cast a looming shadow across my back and on the facing wall. His energy was so strong I felt queasy and weak.

"The human must leave. Von cannot reserve what energy he has left as long as she is here," he said gruffly.

The *human*? He said that like I was some inferior creature. It was obvious that being the Domina Lumen meant nothing to him, even if I hadn't proven myself to the Lumen yet.

"I'm not leaving Von." I turned and faced Gutar in a rare moment of bravery, hoping it wouldn't be my last.

Amara stepped between us. "Ysolde, before you do something stupid, I must warn you. Gutar is a barbarian. He comes from a violent place. He has been a leader in our world for centuries and has seen humans at their worst. Humans are spineless and greedy and have no respect for their planet in his eyes."

"I'm not like other humans."

"It doesn't matter that you are the Domina Lumen. He won't protect you. He and his tribe are the protectors of the Lumen. He has come only to help us, not you."

I looked directly into his cold eyes. He stared at me with disgust. Something inside of me wanted to prove him wrong. I knew Von would not be in the state he was in if I hadn't foolishly gone to Kraegon's lair. But I had to get Dan, so where was I supposed to draw the line on what was right and wrong? Gutar would have left Dan to die. That wasn't an option for me.

"You should go before the sun sets, Ysolde."

Amara opened the door to show me out.

"The last thing we need is more helpless humans wandering around the woods at night."

I didn't like the way she said that. Amara was beginning to sound more like Gutar than Von's sister. I needed her on my side.

"Will you be alright?" I asked Von quietly. My heart ached for him to be strong again. This was my fault. I should be the one lying on the cold floor, not him.

"I'll be okay," he murmured faintly.

"Kolt will go with you to your Jeep," Amara said.

I looked back at Von one last time. Would I see him again or would Gutar take him back to their world to be replaced by another?

"What about the stone and Von's energy signature? How can we get those back, now?" I asked as I walked out the door.

"One thing at a time. Von is too weak to travel. He is our first priority."

I followed Amara through the cave to the mine shaft entrance. Kolt and I crawled through the tunnel in record time. Nothing could stand in my way now.

16. Detour

Kolt and I ran through the forest toward my Jeep. When we arrived, I knelt down and snuggled my face in his soft fur. He felt warm against my cold cheeks. His bright eyes twinkled as if to say "Good luck!" then he turned and dashed back into the woods.

I drove to Cam's house. The lights were still on, but Cam's truck was gone. Dan was slouched on the couch watching T.V. and eating popcorn. He jumped up when I entered.

"Where in the hell have you been? Did you get your stuff from the dorm?" His voice was tight with anxiety.

"No. Something came up. Sorry to be late. Where's Cam?"

"He's with some girl named Alia."

"What?" I shrieked.

"Alia. Isn't she a friend of yours?"

"No! I can't believe Cam went to see her!"

"Calm down. Geez. She called and said she had a flat tire at the canyon. Cam offered to help."

"You let him go *alone*?"

"What's the big deal? You're not jealous are you?" he chuckled.

"You don't understand. Alia is human, but she's working with Kraegon. She's evil like he is. She has the stone. Cam must be in the middle of a trap to lure me out there!"

"How do you know all this?"

"I just came from the cave with Amara and Von."

"What?"

"You can bitch at me about that later. I found out that Tiff and those girls were killed by Alia and Kraegon!"

"So, Cam could be in trouble?"

"Yes!"

Dan jumped up from the couch and started putting his boots on. "We need to leave, now! Do you have any weapons?"

"Even if we had an arsenal, it wouldn't do any good against those guys. Bullets don't faze them."

"Not true. You said Alia is human. If we captured her and Kraegon knew we could kill her, he might be willing to trade her for Cam. Come on!"

"I'm not going to prison for murder."

"Murder? This is self-defense. We'd be doing the planet a huge favor. Wouldn't you fight for Cam's life?" Dan's strength filled the room.

"Yes, of course! But . . ."

"Then help me find something to fight with!"

I dug into my backpack and pulled out the kitchen knife.

"This is all I have."

"That's better than nothing. Let me see what else I can find."

Dan ran through the house looking for weapons. After a few minutes, he returned with a rusted machete and a baseball bat.

"These will have to do. How are your melee skills?"

"What melee skills?"

"Didn't you take some karate classes back home after that guy you dated got rough with you?"

"I can kick a guy in the groin and break his hold, but this is different, Dan. I don't think energy entities fight like that."

My entire body began to quake. This was it. This was going to be my strongest test so far and it was going to be at the canyon, the place I feared the most.

"The last fight I was in didn't turn out so great," he said. "But this is Cam, dammit. You take the bat and the knife and I'll take the machete. Now, grab your jacket and let's go!"

I had always admired my brother's enthusiasm for taking risks, but this was a life or death situation. A machete, a bat and a kitchen knife against Alia, Kraegon and the Vapors wasn't exactly a winning plan.

We jumped into my Jeep and headed to the canyon with Dan at the wheel. I was terrified. We were doing this without Von, Amara, Kolt and now Gutar. We were nuts, but there was no time to wait for help or for us to run back to the cave.

Night had fallen by the time we arrived at the canyon. Alia had told Dan and Cam her car was in the parking lot near the trail leading to the north rim. It sounded like the same place where she and I and her so-called friends had gone hiking.

I remembered that when Dan and I played our computer game, the element of surprise was the best way to get the winning edge in a player-versus-player experience, but how do you surprise an energy entity?

We turned the Jeep's lights off as we neared the parking lot and drove into the woods, out of sight of anyone there. With weapons in hand, we walked silently through the trees toward the parking area. In the moonlight, I could barely make out a truck and car parked side-by-side up ahead. It was Cam's truck. My heart beat so fast I could barely breathe.

We crouched behind a fallen pine, looking for any movement up ahead. I felt certain that Kraegon could see us in the woods, no matter where he was. I tried to block that horrifying thought and focused on looking for Cam and Alia. Not too far away, I heard the sound of scuffling and rocks falling into the canyon.

"Did you hear that?" I whispered to Dan.

"Hush! I heard it. Stay low and follow me," he whispered back.

Dan was always the leader in-game. He had better instincts for fighting than I did, although I was better at spotting a dangerous situation. My instincts were shouting at me to turn back, but that didn't matter. Cam's life was at stake.

We moved forward toward the sounds, hunching down and trying to look as small as possible. This is when stealth or an invisibility potion would really come in handy. I felt like a giant trying to hide behind pebbles and twigs. My body started shaking involuntarily. The terrifying reality of the moment was catching up with my adrenaline rush which had, up until now, helped me get this far. What were we going to do when we *did* find Cam?

No matter how hard I gripped the wooden bat, I couldn't seem to get a good hold on it. It felt foreign and clumsy in my palm. I'd never used a club weapon or any weapon in real life. I'd played a little softball, but I was better at catching the ball than hitting it. How hard do you have to hit someone to knock them down? Was I even strong enough to do that?

"Down!" Dan whispered, making a strong downward motion with his hand. We both hit the ground. Up ahead were two figures standing near the rim. I assumed they were Alia and Cam. My teeth began to chatter.

"Be quiet!"

"I – can't – help it," I stuttered under my breath. I bit my lip, trying to force my mouth shut. A tear escaped the corner of my eye as I tried to steady my nerves. Where the hell was my courage?

"Okay, here's what we're going to do," Dan said quietly. "We need to split up so we can make a distraction. You go over by that big boulder and make some noise to distract Alia while I move closer to Cam. Don't stay in the same place too long. Keep moving around, but don't get any closer to them and don't go too far, okay?"

"I don't want to go alone," I said, sounding like a little kid.

"Dammit, you have to. Do it for Cam and your buddy Von."

"What will you do?"

"If Alia leaves Cam to check out the noise, I'll run in and grab him. If she takes him with her, I'll attack her from the rear. If Cam can fight, we'll be three against one."

"*If* he's okay." I added.

"If he's not, I don't know what we'll do."

"Great." I felt my energy vanish.

"You have a better idea? I'm all ears."

"We can't do this with just the two of us."

"We can't sit around and wait for your friends to show up either."

"Alia wants *me*, not Cam. Maybe if I walk up to her alone, she'll release Cam and take me, then you and Cam can attack her."

"No way. You really think she's going to release Cam? I think she'll keep both of you then it'll be just me against her. We really ought to just throw her ass over the cliff and be done with it."

"After we get the stone."

"You and that damn stone. Okay, let's do this. You run behind that boulder and pick up a rock. I'll start heading toward Cam. When I do, you throw the rock as far and as hard as you can in the opposite direction. Try to hit something that will make a sound to distract Alia."

A sudden strong wind began whipping my hair around in circles. The energy in the air was changing. I looked at Dan apprehensively then started to dash.

He suddenly grabbed my arm and held me back, then he looked up at the sky.

"Wait until the moon goes behind that cloud. Wait just another second. Okay, go!"

He let go of my sleeve. I began slinking through the trees while keeping one eye on Alia in the distance.

When I glanced back at Dan, I could no longer see him. Surely he wasn't already heading toward Cam. I hurried to the big boulder, picked up a rock the size of a baseball and hurled it as hard as I could toward a tree. It hit, creating a hollow sound that echoed back toward me. I peeked out to see if Alia had taken the bait. She was still standing on the rim with Cam.

"Dammit," I whispered out loud. I knelt down and nervously groped along the rough ground for another rock. This time I threw it harder and a little to the left of the last one toward a boulder. It hit the large rock with a loud crack. Surely she heard that. I peered around the boulder and saw Alia walking toward the sound holding Cam in front of her for a shield. I drew in a deep breath.

Out of the corner of my eye, I saw Dan sprinting toward Alia. This was it! I hesitated for a moment, gripping the bat in my sweaty palm, then charged out to run with Dan. Cam heard our footsteps and stopped. He jerked Alia backwards towards him. Alia turned to face us just as Dan leapt upon her, knocking her to the ground. Alia struggled to get up, clawing and scratching at Dan's face. Cam grabbed her legs as she tried to kick free. They began dragging her toward the rim.

"Get the stone!" I yelled.

"We'll hold her while you get it!" Dan yelled back.

I caught up with the guys and started grappling around on Alia's body, searching for the familiar, round rock that had become such a part of my life. Alia was writhing like a wild animal caught in a net. She raised her head from the dirt and spat in my face.

"Go to hell, Alia!" I screamed, as I continued digging through her pockets and clothes. "Turn her over. It must be in her back pocket!"

Cam and Dan wrangled with her body until they were able to flip her over with a thud, knocking the wind out of her.

"I found it!" I cried, as I forced my hand inside her jean pocket. My voice became strong and loud with confidence as I held the precious stone up for everyone to see.

"Bra – vo," boomed a sarcastic voice in the air. Then slow, intentional clapping echoed through the depths of the canyon.

I froze. "It's Kraegon," I whispered to Cam and Dan.

"Who?" Cam looked at me puzzled.

"He's evil," I said.

"You didn't really think you were going to get out of here alive, did you?" Kraegon's voice bellowed. Alia chuckled while spitting dirt from her mouth. Cam still had her face planted on the ground.

Dan tightened his vise grip on her arms. "Shut up!" he yelled, jerking her to her feet. He and Cam dragged her away from the rim where Kraegon's voice seemed to be coming from.

The moon bathed the area in tones of grays. We watched Kraegon materialize from the mouth of the canyon. He was walking on air, just as I had seen in my dreams.

"What the hell?" Cam stuttered, staring at him.

"Let's end this little party once and for all, shall we?" Kraegon raised his arms to the night sky. The wind picked up, swirling dust into the air in a huge vortex. Other humanoids started appearing from nowhere. They stood next to him in the air. I recognized their figures as the friends Alia and I went hiking with. There was an additional new female. The group of Vapors walked through the air toward us, landing on the rim.

"I believe you have met my friends, Jesse, Jon and Magdeline. My sister has decided to join me in my efforts. Kikka, this is Ysolde, the Domina Lumen, as her precious Von likes to call her." Kikka smiled wickedly.

I remembered that Von had Kikka's energy signature and had traded it to Kraegon for Dan's life. She had the same cold eyes as Kraegon. Her face was young and beautiful with pale skin and long, black hair. She was a terrifying ghostly image as she hovered above the canyon in midair, her black gown billowing from the updrafts.

Kraegon chuckled. "Jesse and his friends are good at masquerading as humans. Much like your precious Von is, or should I say *was*." I held my breath. "It's too bad he couldn't attend. I love a good challenge. But this little show you three are putting on is an annoyance. Need I say more?"

Kraegon was looking in my direction with a cold stare. His eyes became white and empty. I felt my entire body start to stiffen. My feet became rooted to the ground as he approached. The fingers in my hand holding Athas involuntarily straightened, causing the stone to fall to the ground next to my boot. Dan and Cam seemed to be frozen in place just like me.

Alia rose from the ground and dusted herself off. She bent down and retrieved the stone, making sure to look me squarely in the eye with a smirk as she passed by heading toward Kraegon.

"Which one should I take first?" he asked. I could hear Dan and Cam trying to move their feet amid the rocks and dirt as he approached calmly. "I think it's only fitting for the new one to go. I don't know him." Kraegon pointed toward Cam. "He means nothing to me."

"That's Cam. The stupid, gullible one," Alia laughed.

I could hear Cam trying to say something to Alia, but only muffled noises came from his frozen mouth.

"Humans," Kraegon sneered, "aren't they *all* stupid and gullible?" He raised a crystal in Cam's direction. The crystal began to glow bright red, emitting a static charge. Wisps of my hair began rising toward the sky as if something invisible was pulling each strand upward. I heard crackling sounds of electricity then felt a strong shift in the air pressure. My ears popped, and suddenly Cam was gone.

"Good-bye, Cam," Kraegon said nonchalantly, placing the crystal into his pocket. "He'll make a nice snack for later. Now, who's next?"

17. BATTLE

"Cam!" I tried to scream, but nothing came out. My facial muscles were hard as stone.

Cam was innocent in all this. He had been used as bait. His only guilt was being my friend. Why didn't they just take me and get it over with.

Kraegon pointed a crystal at Dan. I wrenched my eyes in his direction. He glared at Kraegon with a fire of defiance. The crystal began to glow red. Static electricity filled the air.

A distant sound suddenly came from the direction of the road leading to the parking lot. Mags and Kikka turned their heads to look. My ears strained to hear the high pitched hissing sound coming closer. Kraegon paused and lowered the crystal. I watched as he stared into the dark toward the road.

The hissing grew louder, then it stopped. The canyon became quiet again except for the wind forcing its way through the pine boughs. Was another entity coming? I didn't think they made any sound when they popped in and out of dimensions and they certainly didn't drive cars.

I kept my eyes on Kraegon. He turned back toward Dan as if nothing had changed and raised the crystal again. It began to glow and emit a charge.

I knew it would only be a few minutes before Dan would be put back in a crystal again. I waited for the air pressure to change. There was a loud crack of thunder. A lightning bolt blasted a tree close to Jesse, Mags and Jon. They jumped back. Another one hit near Kraegon, causing him to drop the crystal. I would've been running for my life if I could have moved. Lightning began striking all around us, herding Kraegon and his group away from the rim, toward the parking lot.

The lightning seemed to be intentionally placed to keep Kraegon from going back to his lair in the canyon. I remembered Von had said lightning could be a death sentence for an energy entity. It all depended on the charge. Positive lightning could kill Kraegon. Negative lightning could kill Von. I knew it would be a certain death sentence for me no matter.

A warm surge of energy suddenly wrapped around my body. Tiny beads of sweat began to form on my forehead. I felt Von's presence, but how could that be?

"I'm here." His low, confident voice whispered from behind. "Don't be afraid."

Von! I couldn't say it, but I felt it in every inch of my being. Von's face emerged from the dark, his ice blue eyes gazed into mine. My heart flushed. He placed his hands on my shoulders. Suddenly, I could move again.

"I thought you were too weak to travel. I can't believe you're here." I breathed a momentary sigh of relief. "Kraegon has Cam in a crystal."

"Gutar and the others are here," he said. "There's going to be a battle. We'll need your help to get the stone from Alia. Be careful. Energy shards will be cast. If you're struck by one, you will be killed."

"My death seems to be imminent anyway."

"No, Ysolde. We're here for you. Just remember what I said."

"But, how can you fight without your energy signature?"

"I can't go into my energy form, but I can still fight."

Von walked over to Dan still frozen in place and put his hands on Dan's shoulders. He fell to the ground then quickly stood up.

"Thanks," he said. "Let's go get Cam!"

Von motioned for us to follow him. We ran toward Amara, Kolt and Gutar in the parking lot.

The battle had already begun. Horizontal flashes of light were flying back and forth between the two groups. Jesse, Jon and Mags were standing at the opposite end of the lot. Kraegon and Gutar were throwing lightning spears at each other, like a duel between wizards.

Von clutched my hand tightly. His devotion to my safety and the stone gave me strength and courage. I scanned the area, trying to see Alia amid the flashes of light.

Jesse and Jon were to our right at a distance. They saw me and came running in my direction. I started to run toward the woods. Von pulled me back.

"Don't move!" he yelled. "Stay here!"

He let go of my hand and ran toward Jesse and Jon, causing them to change course. He thrust his arms forward. A silver river of energy charged from his hands towards Jon, knocking him onto the ground.

Out of the corner of my eye, I saw Kolt bounding across the lot, dodging the energy bolts. He leapt onto Jesse, tearing pieces of flesh from his human shell. Beams of light began oozing from his body. Jesse picked Kolt up and flung him onto the ground. Kolt got back up, shook his fur then leapt onto Jesse again, this time attacking his face. He ripped a chunk from his cheek. Jesse's energy radiated out of the wound making his face look like a glowing sphere with hanging flesh.

Dan and I were vulnerable standing on the edge of the parking lot without Von. I didn't know what to do. I turned toward Dan. He was spellbound, watching the entities battle each other with weapons straight out of science fiction. Gutar and Amara were aiming straight for Kraegon with their energy bolts. Mags was standing near Kraegon. I caught a glimpse of Alia hiding behind them.

My eyes shifted back toward Von and Kolt who had Jesse cornered in front of two huge boulders. Von threw his hands forward. An energy shard hit Jesse throwing him against the rocks. Before he could get up, Von and Kolt hit him with more energy at the same time. There was a loud popping sound and Jesse vanished.

Jon became enraged and leapt on Kolt. He lifted the white wolf above his head and heaved him against another boulder. Kolt's body hit hard. He crumpled to the ground. I watched, waiting for him to get up. He lay still, lifeless.

Von ran to Kolt and knelt beside him briefly then stood up and bolted toward Jon. Kolt didn't move. I wanted to run to him. I looked at Gutar, hoping he could help. He was completely consumed with keeping Kraegon away from everyone else.

I grabbed Dan by the hand. He was in some kind of a daze. I jerked him toward me. When he looked in my direction, his pupils were glowing white. I gasped in horror. He had the same eyes Kraegon had in my dream.

"What's wrong with your eyes?" I shouted over the thunderous booms of the energy bolts streaming through the air nearby.

"I don't know."

"They're glowing."

"They are? I'm okay," he muttered quietly without emotion. Like hell he was. Something was horribly wrong.

"Come with me!" I pulled him into the woods away from the battle. We had to get Alia. I was now the leader. I hated being the leader of a group when I played computer games. I didn't want the responsibility of the group's lives even if they were just avatars. I was much better at following orders than giving them. I didn't want to be in charge of Dan's safety, but I had no choice.

We ran through the woods behind Kraegon and Mags. Dan followed me like a lost dog. Kraegon and Gutar were still casting energy bolts at each other. They both were surrounded by spheres of light like shields preventing either one from taking damage.

Dan and I stopped behind a tree. He stared at me with his translucent eyes. He wasn't capable of defending himself. I had no idea what was going on, but I needed him to be normal again.

"You stay here. I'm going to find Alia," I said. Dan nodded. I crawled behind rocks and bushes and edged my way closer behind Kraegon and Mags. Alia had been right behind them, but she was gone.

I'd have to dowse to find her even though I knew my dowsing under pressure was not to be trusted. How could I clear my mind out here? There was no way I could wander around and body dowse. I'd have to use my pendulum in near-zero visibility.

I unclasped my crystal and held it close to my body. My first question was to see if Alia was even in this area. The crystal responded yes. Was Alia within fifty feet of me? Again, it responded yes. I asked it to swing in Alia's direction. The crystal swung clockwise briefly then started swinging back and forth. Alia was either directly in front of me or behind me. I asked if Alia was in front. The crystal responded no.

My gut tensed. I froze. I didn't need the pendulum to answer the next question, I could feel it. The hair on the back of my neck stood up in full alarm. I knew Alia was right behind me.

My hand quietly pushed the pendant safely down inside my pocket. I no longer had the bat. The kitchen knife was in my backpack somewhere in the woods. I slowly bent down and grabbed a large rock, then prepared to fight Alia to the death.

18. Death

I felt Alia's warm breath as she let out a low, evil chuckle. She knew I was terrified. I tightened my grip on the rock, took a step forward then swung around, striking with all my strength in her direction. Alia parried my blow, moving out of the way. I fell to the ground, hitting nothing but air.

She laughed at me. "A rock? Seriously?" She stood in front of me as I struggled to stand up. To my shock and terror, there was Dan standing next to her, grinning. The glowing in his eyes was more intense now. He stared at me in silence.

"What have you done to my brother?"

"He's one of us, now."

"He would *never* join you! Dan! Wake up!" I yelled at him in disbelief, my eyes pleading for him to respond. He stood motionless, like a zombie.

"Take her weapon," ordered Alia. Dan moved toward me, his hand grasped the rock.

"Stop!" I yelled, jerking it away from him and stepping back a few feet. "Dan, it's Ysolde, your sister!"

"Get her," said Alia calmly.

I quickly turned and began to run. Dan was right behind me.

"Alia is using you. I'll help you, Dan, I promise!" I yelled back at him as I ran faster through the woods in the direction of Von.

When I arrived at the parking lot, I looked back and could see Dan's eyes glowing eerily in the forest, not far behind. I ran to the area where Gutar and Amara had been fighting Kraegon, but they were no longer there. No Lumen or Vapors were in the area except for Kolt's body, still lying on the ground. Had everyone else been disintegrated? Did they take their battle to another dimension? Was I left here alone with Dan and Alia?

I listened for the sounds of battle. Faint noises were coming from the rim of the canyon. I could see Dan sprinting across the parking lot, aiming right for me. I headed toward the rim.

I stopped a few yards from the precipice. Kraegon and Gutar were floating in air above the gorge, still deadlocked in aerial combat. I didn't see Mags. Amara and Von were fighting Kikka and Jon on the ground nearby. The time for me to think and worry about my safety was over. I ran toward Von, dodging energy shards flying in every direction.

Just as I had almost reached Von, Dan caught up with me. He tackled me to the ground from behind. Alia was not far away. I struggled to get up, but he held me down, smashing my face into the dirt.

"Help!" I screamed. Von spun around, turning toward my voice. He saw me on the ground with Dan on top and

Alia closing in fast. Dan yanked me up off the ground in front of him to use as a shield against Von. I struggled to pull free, violently twisting my body, but his hold was too strong.

Von looked stunned. I was sure he was confused. Seeing Dan holding me for Alia was crazy. My brother, my blood-born protector was now aiding in my death. Von was my guardian and he would do whatever was necessary to keep me safe, but would that include harming Dan?

"Ysolde!" Von yelled.

Alia leaped into the air and landed nearby. "You're all mine, now," she sneered, raising the machete and moving in for the kill.

My body flinched as I prepared for the long rusted blade to slice through my flesh. Dan gripped my wrists tighter until they burned with pain.

"Dan! You're hurting me! Let go!"

Furia suddenly emerged within me. I knew I was going to have to hurt Dan to get away. I kicked him as hard as I could in the groin.

"Ahhh!" he cried, releasing his grip. He stumbled to the ground in pain. I ducked just as Alia lowered the machete, missing my head by inches.

She raised the blade again, yelling at Dan, "Get her!"

As I tried to get away, my boots slipped on the loose gravel. I fell, then scrambled to my feet and ran toward Von.

"Ysolde! Get down!" yelled Von as he raised his hands to cast an energy shard. I slammed into the dirt. Alia was closing in fast and to my horror, Dan was right behind her.

Von let go a river of energy shards in Alia's direction. She saw them coming and dropped to the ground, causing the shards to go over her and hit Dan directly in the chest. He instantly crumpled to the earth, lying motionless.

"No, Von! Stop!" I screamed. "Oh, God! No!" I cried, running back toward Dan.

"Stay down!" Von shouted as he aimed again at Alia. She made a dash for the rim and leapt off the edge just as Von's energy hit her, then she disappeared into the void.

"The stone!" I yelled. But Dan was more important. I rushed to his side. Dan's face was tranquil and silent. His eyes were open. They had gone back to blue, but without the spark of life. I leaned my head down toward his mouth to feel if he was breathing. No air was coming out. I put my fingers on his neck to feel for a pulse. There was nothing. I frantically began pumping his chest and blowing into his mouth over and over, but it was too late.

I cradled Dan's head in my arms, stroking his face. "Dan, come back! Please, come back. I'm sorry. I'm sorry. It's all my fault." Tears streamed down my face.

Von hurried over and knelt beside me. I couldn't make myself look at him. He killed my brother. I didn't care if it was an accident or if he was trying to protect me. The rage inside me boiled over. Dan was dead. No more laughter, no more joking around or playing games, no more having someone I could depend on. He was the last of my family except for Oma. How could he be gone?

I hated Von.

Von's distressed face said it all. He knew Dan's death was his fault. He placed his fingers on the inside of Dan's wrist to feel for a pulse. After a few seconds he removed his hand, looking down at the ground.

"Bring him back. Can't you bring him back?" I moaned.

"Alia was going to kill you." He touched my shoulder gently. "I'm sorry."

I jerked his hand away. "You killed him! You killed him! You're a killer! All of you are killers!" I sobbed. "Sorry won't bring him back. Don't you understand? I don't care about living if Dan isn't in my life."

"You don't mean that, Ysolde, I understand your pain."

"How can you possibly understand my pain? You're not human. You don't have a heart. You're just a mass of energy. The last being I want in my life right now is you." I buried my head in Dan's chest

"I *do* know how you feel. I lost someone who was very dear to me once. Her name was also Ysolde. Your ancestor. I loved her and Kraegon killed her. I never meant to hurt Dan. Please forgive me."

"So that's why you feel so close to me? Because I have *her* name?" I raised my head, glaring at him.

"No. I care for you because of who *you* are."

"Leave me alone. I don't want anything to do with the Lumen. Kraegon can have the damn stone, wherever it is."

191

"What about your grandmother? She needs you. The Lumen need you. You are their only hope to rid Earth and our world within of Kraegon."

"You leave Oma out of this! I told you, I don't care about the Lumen or that damn stone anymore. Go away!" I hugged Dan's body never wanting to let go.

This entire tragic event was my fault. I wish I had never known about the stone. I wish I'd been born in a normal family. I'd be living a normal college life in the dorm, giving crazy parties with Tiff, hanging out with Cam, hiking in the mountains, playing in the snow, playing the game with Dan. That was all over now. I sank into my angry, mournful thoughts, oblivious to the battle that was still raging nearby.

Von stood up and walked back toward the battle. His head and shoulders were bent forward with a look of defeat. I held Dan as I watched him walk away.

"That's right, Von. Go ahead and leave," I said quietly. "I don't need you anymore. I don't need anyone."

I wiped the dirt from Dan's face and leaned down and kissed his cool, pale cheek. It was the first time I had ever kissed him.

"I love you. I'm sorry that I never told you that." I stroked his wild blonde hair. "I know that you knew it, though. We didn't have to say it to each other, did we? We always knew what the other was thinking." I laid my head back down on his chest and closed my eyes, no longer sobbing, now just numb. My mind drifted silently among heavy black clouds.

Abysmal canyon was the death of my entire family now except Oma. I wanted nothing more to do with it. I would take Dan's body back to Texas and never return to Colorado again. Oma would either forgive me or not. I didn't care. And the Lumen? Let them fight their own battles.

A strong, male voice suddenly spoke from the forest shadows nearby. "Get the stone."

I raised my head off Dan's chest and looked around in the cold night air, but saw no one.

"Get the stone!" the man's voice said again, this time louder and more insistent.

"Who's there?" I called. My eyes strained to see.

"Get up and stop feeling sorry for yourself. Get the stone and get Cam. He needs you."

"Who the hell are you?" Only silence responded. The wind picked up. Small particles of dust blew into my eyes.

"Get up!" the voice bellowed. A loud clap of thunder followed nearby.

"I'm not leaving my brother!" I yelled back.

"You won't be leaving him, because I'm right here." Dan suddenly appeared in front of me.

"Wha . . . ? Dan?" I looked down at his dead body. "It can't be you."

"Why not?" His eyes were a brilliant ice blue and his hair was white blonde, just like Von. He looked very much alive.

"Because, you're dead? How can you be alive and dead at the same time?" I stood up and backed away from him, thinking this might be one of Kraegon's tricks.

"Seriously, Ysolde, you can be so dense sometimes. Think about it for a sec."

"Are you Dan's *ghost*?"

"Hell no! Do I look like a ghost? I can't believe you haven't figured this out," Dan's clone chuckled with a big grin.

"You sound like Dan, you look like him, you even act like him, but the real Dan is lying at my feet very dead."

"Listen closely. I'm an en-ti-ty."

"A what?"

"A Lumen?" Dan sighed. "You know, like Von and the others?"

"Are you kidding me?"

"Nope."

"But, how do I know you're not one of Kraegon's Vapors using Dan's body?"

"Ask me a question only Dan would know."

I thought about our childhood and all the crazy things Dan did.

"Okay, what did you drink when you were ten that made you so sick you had to go to the hospital?"

"That's easy. I drank a whole bottle of apple cider vinegar."

"That's right. But, how did you become a Lumen?"

194

"When I died, I was floating in this weird black space. Gutar came out of nowhere and asked if I'd like to join the Lumen. I can't turn down a chance for adventure and I'm not the angel type anyway, so here I am."

"I thought Gutar was fighting Kraegon. How could he be in two places at once?"

"He was fighting Kraegon and still is. I guess he can multi-task," Dan laughed. "It was Von's idea, the invitation, I mean."

"Von was there, too?"

"Your boyfriend was there just long enough to convince Gutar to accept me as one of their own. Gutar's not real keen on humans, but I guess he could always use more Lumen to help fight the Vapors. I'll be the youngest in the family by a few centuries." His eyes lit up with excitement.

"You know Von killed you, don't you?"

"Yeah, he apologized. He's pretty torn up about that. But, it was an accident and he did get rid of Alia. So far, being Lumen doesn't feel that different from human."

My shock over Dan's real death was still fresh. But knowing that he was back and apparently in good form, even if he was a Lumen now, softened my resentment toward Von. He cared enough about us to keep us together. Perhaps I could forgive him, in time.

"That body on the ground is just a shell," Dan said, looking at his corpse. "The Lumen let it stay for your sake, but now that you know about me, it's time to disintegrate it."

"No! I mean, don't we need to take it back to Oma for a funeral?"

"What for? No one back home needs to know I'm dead. I look normal, don't I?"

"Well yeah, I guess, except your hair is white."

"Then don't worry. I'll tell Oma. She'll probably think it's kind of neat. It'll be easier for me to keep an eye on her now. There's so much to learn. I'll be in training for a while. This is going to be so cool!"

"I'm just glad you're alive, or whatever."

"We need to find the stone. Then we have to get Cam's crystal and Von's energy signature from Kraegon then banish him from this world forever. So much to do! Let's go save Cam!" Dan sprinted toward the rim. His courage and enthusiasm had increased tenfold it seemed.

"Wait! I don't know where the stone is."

Dan stopped and turned toward me. "Well, I imagine it fell in the river at the bottom of the canyon when Alia was nuked in mid-air. Now it's up to you, dear Domina Lumen, to dowse for it."

"That's just upriver from where Mom and Dad died."

"I know. I'll be there with you. I'm one of your guardians now."

"You? My guardian? My brother, the newbie recruit is going to save me from doom?"

"And my sis, the Domina Lumen is going to save the planet?"

"Good point. Let's go."

We climbed down the switchbacks that led to the bottom of the canyon and the Dragon's Tongue River where we thought Athas would be. The moonlight was barely enough to see the steep, narrow trail. I cautiously walked sideways to keep my boots from sliding off the edge. Dan leaped down the path ahead, bounding and skipping like a little kid.

By the time we got to the bottom, my thigh muscles were quivering so badly I could barely walk. Abysmal canyon was 2000 feet deep and I had felt every step of the way down. I looked up at the rim. The trees along the edge looked like toy trees an inch tall. The rushing sound of the river echoed within the steep canyon walls. It was eerie and dark and cold in the deep, narrow gorge.

The river was just a few yards away. The current was wild and swift. I hoped I wouldn't have to body dowse in the water. I inhaled deeply, cleared my mind then paced along the water's edge waiting for a tingling sensation. Dan walked beside me. After about a quarter of a mile, I stopped.

"It's no use. I can't do it. There are *thousands* of black rocks down here. How can I distinguish one from the other at night?"

"See that lightning up there on the rim?" Dan asked. "Von, Amara and Gutar are still fighting *for you*. Do it for Kolt. Do it for Cam and Oma."

He was right. Everyone was risking their lives for me. How could I give up? I continued walking, this time closing out all sounds except the sound of the river racing across the rocks. I held the image of the stone with its etched lines in my mind. Every nerve in my body was open for any kind of signal.

I stopped for a moment and closed my eyes. A slight tingling began in my left pinkie finger. It wasn't much, but I concentrated on it as I began walking into the cold water. The current pushed me back and forth. I strained to keep from falling. The tingling became stronger. I took a few more steps then suddenly, my entire body felt an electric jolt.

I plunged both hands into the swirling black water and let my fingers graze over the cold stones below until my fingertips touched something warm. I knew it instantly. Shivers ran up my arm. I fished the stone out of the river and held it up to the moonlight to make sure. Yes, there were the familiar lines carved into the surface. There was Athas. I had done it!

"Took you long enough!" Dan teased from the water's edge. "Now hurry up! There's no time to waste!"

We climbed all the way back up to the rim, stopping several times to let me catch my breath. When we reached the top, we hiked to the woods away from the fighting. Dan stopped me from going further.

"I think you should try to do your magic with the stone from here, out of harm's way. If you get too close to Kraegon, he'll be able to take the stone from you again."

"I don't know what to do." I caressed Athas in my palm.

"Kraegon can't handle positive energy and there's a storm coming. What if you channeled all the positive lightning in the area to hit him at once?"

"Are you nuts? I don't know how to channel lightning! That sounds like something Gutar could do, not me."

"He's not powerful enough by himself. While you're holding Athas, visualize the lightning channeling toward one target."

"And how do you suddenly know all of this?"

"I have no idea. I just do."

"But what if it backfires and hits me instead?"

"It won't, if you visualize it hitting Kraegon, *duh*. Trust yourself, Ysolde."

Just then lightning struck near the edge of the canyon. Drops of rain began to hit the dirt. I could see Kraegon hovering over the abyss. Gutar was standing on the rim, surrounded by a shield of light.

I held Athas in front of my chest and closed my eyes. My mind visualized the lightning coming together into one massive energy bolt striking Kraegon. I opened my eyes. Nothing had happened.

"This is stupid," I said. "It's not going to work."

"I'm not going to baby you like Von does. Remember, this guy killed Mom and Dad. Try again!"

I held Athas toward the sky and visualized all the lightning in the area coming together in one huge energy bolt surrounded by white light. I hurled the massive energy shard in my mind at Kraegon with all the anger I felt toward him.

The air filled with static electricity, then I heard a crackling sound and a sonic boom shook the earth.

"You did it!" cried Dan.

I opened my eyes and saw Kraegon being pummeled by lightning that appeared to be coming from Athas! The stone was glowing white, emitting solid streams of energy toward him. I continued to hold Athas in the air, concentrating on the vision while I watched what was happening.

Jon, Mags and Kikka were shooting bolts at Amara and Von. Dan threw his arms forward toward Jon. Energy steamed from his hands, hitting Jon in the chest. He disintegrated in a cloud of sparks.

"Woo Hoo!" Dan cheered.

Dan ran toward the others while throwing his arms out in midair, aiming at Mags. "Take that!" he shouted. It was as if his character in the game had come to life as a warrior/wizard hybrid.

Mags threw shards in his direction. He dodged the first. The second hit him in the leg. "Ahhh!" he screamed. Rivers of light began beaming from his wound.

"Dan needs help!" I shouted toward Amara. She turned away from Kraegon and saw Mags coming in for the kill on Dan. She threw her arms out with energy and landed a death blow. A puff of sparks followed a loud pop and Mags was gone.

"You're my angel!" Dan yelled to Amara as he jumped up and began channeling energy toward Kraegon.

Kikka moved next to Kraegon. I focused the lightning to hit both targets as one.

"You will regret this, Ysolde!" yelled Kraegon.

"Give us the crystal with the human and Von's energy signature or we will destroy you!" Gutar's voice echoed.

"I will kill the old Domina Lumen, your grandmother, Ysolde!" warned Kraegon.

I couldn't believe what I'd just heard. Oma was back in Texas, alone with no guardian. She would be easy prey for Kraegon.

"Wait!" My concentration dropped. Athas stopped emitting energy. I slowly lowered the stone as the lightning aimed at Kraegon dissipated.

"Ysolde, what are you doing? Why did you stop?" cried Dan.

"I'm protecting Oma." I knew I was failing by not killing Kraegon, but I couldn't risk Oma's life.

Gutar walked forward, his energy stream locked onto Kraegon. "Amara, shield me!" he shouted.

"No! Stop, Gutar!" I screamed.

Amara changed her stance, focusing on protecting Gutar. A vortex of sparks began swirling around him. Holding a long, glowing sword, he walked toward Kraegon.

Then suddenly an explosion of light beamed down from the sky engulfing Gutar, Kraegon and Kikka. A huge black dragon appeared. It descended quickly toward them with talons spread wide. The dragon snatched Kraegon and Kikka then vanished.

"No!" shouted Gutar, raising his sword toward the sky. His voice roared through the canyon. "Xiomar, you shall not survive!"

19. Fire

"I have not seen Xiomar in centuries," Gutar said, staring into the night sky where the black dragon had disappeared. The storm had passed. Stars were peaking from behind the few clouds that remained.

"Who is he?" Dan asked.

"He is the protector of the Vapors," said Gutar.

I looked at Von. "Did you hear Kraegon? He's going to kill Oma! We have to go to Texas and save her."

"Kraegon and Kikka have fled back to their energy world to regenerate. We must go to their world now, while they are weak," Gutar said.

"No, we need to save Oma first!"

Gutar glared at me as though I were the enemy.

"Ysolde, it's like Gutar said, Kraegon needs to regenerate. He's weak and vulnerable right now," Dan said. "He's probably not even thinking about Oma. We need to get Cam back before it's too late."

"But, Oma is *family*. How could you risk her life like that?"

Dan looked away, avoiding my eyes.

"Kraegon has Von's energy signature," Amara said to the group. "There are more reasons to go after Kraegon right now than to save Oma. She's no longer the Domina Lumen."

I felt my jaw tighten. I walked over to Amara and looked her sternly in the face.

"Oma took care of Athas and helped the Lumen for over sixty years. She sacrificed a normal life for you. She lost her daughter, *my* mother, because of you and I lost my father because of you and now you're just going to throw Oma away as if she meant *nothing?*"

I couldn't hide my anger and pain. There was no good solution. Either Oma was going to die or Cam was. We couldn't save both. Even Dan was on their side to go to Kraegon first. Cam was like family and I knew he needed to be saved, but how could Dan choose Cam over his grandmother, our only living relative left?

I looked at Von. "Think about how many times Oma has helped the Lumen in the past. How much she has meant to you. Doesn't that count for something?"

He sighed deeply. "We'll go to Texas and get Oma, *then* we will go to Kraegon."

"Thank you," I said quietly.

"What?" said Amara to Von. "You do realize you're choosing to save a human over killing Kraegon, don't you? You're not thinking like a Lumen, brother. You're thinking like an overly sympathetic human."

"We will go to Kraegon as soon as we have Oma. End of discussion."

Amara walked away, shaking her head.

"Then I will not join you," said Gutar. "By the time you get to Kraegon he will have regenerated. It will be too late to destroy him."

"We need you with us," Von said.

"I do not protect humans. I will return to our world. When you are ready to attack Kraegon, I will return. But as I said, it will be too late."

"Very well." Von walked over next to me. My skin felt a warm surge.

"What about Kolt?" I asked, looking at his limp white body lying in the dirt.

Gutar knelt down beside him. He held his hands out in front with one palm above the other leaving a space between. A small energy orb gradually materialized in his hand, then he placed it inside Kolt's mouth. A few minutes later, Kolt's tail began to thump up and down on the ground.

"Kolt!" I ran to his side and stroked his fur. "I thought you had been killed."

He sat up and began licking my face gently.

"That's enough, Kolt," Amara said, firmly.

"*Never* enough," I said, scratching him behind his ears.

"Ysolde, if you will create a vortex, the others will be able to go to Texas at once," said Von.

"The others? What about you?"

"I can't travel in the energy lines without my energy signature. I have other transportation. You'll be coming with me."

I dreaded trying to find a positive energy line for the vortex under such pressure. I began walking around the area, waiting for warm tingling sensations to occur somewhere in my body. Everyone was watching and waiting. I suspected they were going to be especially critical of me now that I had gotten my way and we were going to save Oma first. Von had crossed a line when he chose me over the Lumen. I felt Gutar's eyes staring a hole through my back. My concentration faded.

"Damn human," Gutar grumbled. He walked to a spot a few yards from where I was standing. "Here is a line!" He glared at me with impatience, pointing at the ground near him.

I hurried to the spot and felt the energy coming up. I held the stone in the proper position and turned it. Nothing happened. "*Come on*," I said under my breath. My hands were shaking from nerves. I tried again. Finally the air began to warp. I felt the familiar dizziness then the vortex appeared. Gutar immediately leaped in as if he couldn't wait to get away from me.

Amara stood next to the portal and turned to Dan. "You coming?"

"Just a sec," he said. He picked me off my feet with a bear hug then dropped me back on the ground.

"I think you're right about going to Oma first," he said. "Cam will be okay until we can get to Kraegon's world. Don't let these guys get to you."

I smiled and whispered in his ear, "Thanks, bro. I'll see you there."

"Don't forget to bring Furia," he grinned. I knew what he meant. Bring my courage.

He stepped next to Amara and she took his hand. "Stay close, Dan. Once you enter the vortex it can be disorienting. Kolt will go in then we'll go together."

Kolt barked a goodbye, then leaped into the whirling field and disappeared.

"Here's to adventure!" exclaimed Dan as he and Amara leaned forward and vanished. My heart gripped my chest. I couldn't lose him. I couldn't lose Oma. The supreme amount of faith I needed to have in myself to be Domina Lumen was too much. Too many things depended on my doing the right thing. And now we were all headed to Texas to find Oma probably dead or kidnapped by the Vapors.

I turned the stone and closed the vortex. The canyon was quiet. Von was standing about ten feet away. His eyes shifted away when I looked at him. We no longer had the excuse of the battle to mask our feelings. I knew I needed to forgive him for killing Dan.

"Von, I . . ."

"You'll be riding with me." His voice was somber and steady.

"I could take my Jeep and follow you, if you prefer."

"Your Jeep is too slow. Come."

I walked behind him in awkward silence. We hiked to the edge of the parking lot. There sat an amazing looking motorcycle.

I had never seen a bike like this. I walked over to it and ran my hand along its sleek metal frame. The body looked like a large, elongated, space-age ninja bike. It sat just a few inches above the ground. The front end had low, short handle bars that were close to the frame and required the driver to lean way down to reach them. It had a huge, fat back tire and a small windshield at the front that lay almost horizontally against the frame. The seat was small and snug and not made for two people.

"You won't find these on the street," Von said as he mounted the bike then kicked the kick stand back. "It's an electric drag racer."

"Electric? Is it fast?"

"The fastest in *your* world. You'll need to hang on."

"Won't the battery run out?"

"I have enough energy in my body to keep it charged. I have something for you."

He motioned for me to come closer, then held his hand out. A black snake appeared coiled up in his palm.

"Nix!"

"I've been guarding him. Now that you have Athas back, you need to let him guard the stone again."

I gave the stone to the Nix. He quickly slid up my arm and wrapped himself securely around my neck. It felt good to have him back knowing I wasn't the only one responsible for Athas.

"Get on the bike, Ysolde."

I looked at my minuscule portion of the remainder of the seat behind him. I was going to have to press my body tightly against his to keep from falling off.

I placed one hand on his shoulder then swung my leg over the seat like mounting a short pony. Our bodies were immediately pressed together as one. Von's tall frame and broad shoulders were directly in front of my face. He pushed a button and the motor started with a quiet, hissing sound. It sounded nothing like the usual loud clatter of Dan's old Harley.

"Put your arms around my waist, lean down and hold tight."

I had ridden down the endless straight highways of Texas on the back of Dan's motorcycle many times, but that was a normal seat with a back rest and we weren't going warp speed. I wrapped my arms around Von's waist and pressed my face sideways into his cotton t-shirt. My cheek rubbed against the muscles in his upper back. It was the first time I had been so close to him. His scent was fresh and clean. I felt his magnetism pull me in. Our energies blended together as one. Beads of sweat formed on my forehead.

We leaned way down, almost horizontally. He drove the bike in a small semi-circle to turn it around toward the road then stopped for a moment.

"Ready?" he asked.

"I think so."

I tightened my grip around him. Von placed his warm, strong hand on my cold hands for a brief moment, squeezing them with reassurance then put his hand back on the throttle.

"Here we go." He put the bike in gear with his boot and twisted the throttle. The bike lurched forward. We flew away from the canyon of death at lightning speed.

Through all the "s" curves, my body began to meld with Von's as we leaned left and right in unison. We reached the highway in seconds it seemed. He leaned into the final turn, then we hit a long straight highway and he kicked the bike into high gear. It felt like we were airborne, zipping through an energy tunnel on our way to another dimension.

As the motorcycle droned on, I had time to think about all that was ahead. What would we find in Texas? If Oma was okay, would we take her with us to Kraegon's world? Was Cam still in the crystal or had Kraegon consumed his energy by now? We still had to retrieve Von's energy signature. The list seemed impossible, not to mention the ultimate goal of banishing Kraegon from Earth.

And what about my classes? My new world made those few frustrating days back at the dorm with Tiff and Tanner look like child's play. I knew before I came to college that my priority was meeting Von and taking over the role as Domina Lumen. I just had no idea what that meant.

I tucked my head deeper into Von's back, protecting my face from the cutting wind. He glanced over his shoulder in my direction, his white hair whipping around his face.

"You okay?" he yelled.

I nodded, looking into his bright blue eyes. Our hearts connected for a moment. I nestled my face back into his body and closed my eyes.

We made it to Texas in a quarter of the time it would've taken to drive there in my Jeep. Von didn't need directions to my family home and Oma's Burrow out back. He said he used to watch me working in the garden with Mom, painting in my studio in Dad's workshop, and helping Oma bake medlar pies.

The morning sun was rising above the fields as we turned off the highway onto the long, gravel country road that led to the house. Smoke was rising in the air in the distance. It wasn't unusual to see wildfires this time of the year in Texas.

As we drove nearer, I realized the smoke was coming from the same side of the road as our house. I strained to look around Von. The smoke was thick and black. Burning debris drifted through the air. I heard popping and hissing sounds. This wasn't a grassfire.

When we rounded the last bend, I screamed in horror. My house was engulfed in flames.

"Oma!"

The flames hadn't reached the back of the land where the Burrow was.

"Von! Let me off!"

He stopped the cycle across the road. I leaped off and grabbed my cell phone out of my backpack and called 911. The volunteer fire department said they would get there as soon as they could, but I knew it would be too late to save the house.

We ran back toward the Burrow calling Oma's name. I reached out to open the door. It opened on its own.

"Oma! Thank goodness you're safe!"

I pushed the door farther open. Instead of Oma, Amara's face shone in the dim light by the window with Kolt and Dan standing next to her.

"Dan! Where's Oma?"

He pushed his way past Amara. "She's not here. We looked everywhere."

"What?"

"She left this letter and pouch for you."

He handed me a torn piece of paper and a violet velvet pouch. The handwriting on the paper was hurried and sloppy, not Oma's usual calligraphic penmanship. My hands trembled as I held it toward the window light and read it out loud.

"*Ysolde, inside this pouch is a map and pendulum with a witness chamber. I have placed a lock of my hair in the chamber. Use the pendulum with the map to dowse for my location. Please come as soon as you can. My life is in danger. Love, Oma*"

I pulled the small rolled up map out of the pouch. It showed a strange land I had never seen before.

"Where is this place?"

Von scanned it briefly. "That is the world within."

"The world Oma spoke of? The world inside Earth?"

"Yes."

"But I thought she was just being crazy. I thought that was just another tale. It's impossible for another world to be *inside* Earth."

"Just deal with it, Ysolde," Dan said. "I was shocked, too. I guess all those crazy stories about the earth being hollow with another world inside were true."

"So, I have to map dowse in a world inside this one to find Oma? Are you kidding me? What if I can't find her?"

Dan looked out the window. "The fire is spreading this way! We need to get out of here!"

I hurriedly stuffed the pouch in my backpack then looked toward the main house just as the roof collapsed. It fell onto the second floor where my bedroom was and nearly every material thing I held dear to my heart went up in flames.

Dan grabbed my arm, attempting to pull me away from the only home I'd ever known. The last memories of Mom and Dad were burning into ashes. The family photos. Dad's workshop. Mom's garden. My studio. Oma's Burrow would be next.

"I can't go."

I couldn't move. I couldn't breathe. A part of me wanted to burn with the house. I'd had enough.

"Come on!" He swept me up in his arms and carried me through the field, past the burning house across the road to safety.

"What are we going to do, Dan?" I sat in the grass in shock, watching the house implode into a charred, black mass.

"We're going to that other world to find Oma."

"And just how do we get *inside* the Earth?"

"Energy lines," Von said.

"You can't travel in those without your energy signature, can you?" I asked.

"He can now," Amara said, with a rare grin. "Thanks to your grandmother." She held up a small, glowing orb.

"That looks like the same thing Gutar used to revive Kolt," I said.

"It's similar. It's a temporary energy signature, good for one use. Oma left it for Von."

"And you wanted to let her die," I said, finally getting a shot back at her arrogance. Amara didn't reply. I took that as her way of apologizing.

"Won't you need more than one? What if you get stuck in that other world?" I asked Von.

"All I need is to get there."

"So who's responsible for burning our house down?" Dan asked.

"Probably Kraegon," said Amara. "Another one of his failed attempts to kill your grandmother."

Dan's face flushed with anger.

"Von, where do you think Oma is in that other world?" I asked.

"We'll go to Kalisfaar first. You can map dowse from there."

"I hope you know how to ride a horse and use a sword," Amara smirked. "The world within is quite medieval."

"Furia would be in heaven," I said half-heartedly.

Normally, I'd love to ride a horse again and attempt to use a real sword, but Oma's life was in jeopardy in a strange world where everyone was depending on me to find her. The idea of riding a horse while carrying a heavy sword just added to the stress of the moment.

Amara looked at Von. "Who is *Furia*?"

"Ysolde's avatar when she plays her game."

"Oh, you mean her childish form of escape from reality?" She looked at me with one eyebrow raised.

"Something like that," I said. I didn't have any spare energy to give to her snide comments.

The sound of sirens could be heard in the distance. We watched the fire truck and ambulance speed up the gravel road with clouds of white dust billowing behind them.

"A little late," Dan said.

"At least the Burrow is saved," I said.

"Where will you leave that, Von?" I nodded toward his motorcycle.

"Inside the Burrow for now."

We watched as the firemen dowsed the remains of the house into a wet, smoldering mess then soaked the fields surrounding it, extinguishing the grassfires. Mom's rose garden was burned, but by some miracle, Oma's medlar trees were spared.

After the firemen left, we wheeled Von's cycle into Oma's living room. I grabbed as much survival food as I could stuff into my backpack. There was no telling what kind of food would be available in the medieval world within. Visions of steaming boar's heads on platters made me shudder.

"Think you have enough there, sis?" Dan grinned, trying to lift my spirits as he followed me around Oma's kitchen.

"In case you haven't noticed, I'm the only human left in this bizarre little dysfunctional family. I have to eat sometime." I tried to smile back.

"Man, I really miss my munchies."

"Can Lumen eat normal food?"

"I don't think we have a stomach. I think we're just a bunch of energy inside." He put his hand on his mid-section and felt around.

"So I guess crystals are your yummy munchies now."

"Yay," he said, unenthusiastically.

We walked out of the Burrow and locked the door behind us. I hid the key in a jar buried near a medlar tree, one of Oma's many secret hiding places.

"Time to go," said Von. "You'll need to open another vortex for us, Ysolde."

"How do I know where to go once we're in the vortex?"

"Just hold my hand. I'll lead the way."

"As you enter the vortex, think *Kalisfaar*," Amara said to Dan. "Your thoughts will guide you to your destination."

I reached up to take Athas from Nix. He let the stone gently slide into my hand. The field near the house had been one of my dowsing training grounds with Oma. I knew where most of the energy lines were. I walked to the closest one. A strong tingling sensation came up through my feet and into my body.

"This is the line."

Everyone gathered nearby. The air reeked of wet, burnt grass and wood, melted plastic and metal. Our family home lay in drowned, black ruins. I thought about the little wooden horse Dad had carved for me sitting next to my bed in my room. I wasn't there to save it. Tears welled in my eyes.

I held Athas in my palm then turned the stone clockwise. It only took a few seconds for the dizziness to come this time. The air began to warp back and forth then the vortex opened.

I looked at my new family. Was I the only one who regretted leaving my Earth home? Kolt licked my hand as if he had read my mind. I stroked his head a few times then he leaped into the void.

Amara grabbed Dan's hand. "See you there, sis," he said as they jumped into the opening in unison.

That left just the two of us again. I gave Athas to Nix and felt him wrap his tail securely around the stone. Von stood next to the portal.

"Are you ready?"

I gazed into his eyes then back at the steaming ashes of my former life. He touched my chin, gently pulling my face back to his.

"Oma is waiting. She needs you."

"I know. It's just . . ."

"You've shown great courage, Ysolde. You have your memories. No one can take those from you."

Von took the energy orb Oma had left for him and placed it in his mouth. His skin began to turn translucent. His body filled with radiant energy as his image transformed into Lumen. The glowing humanoid form held his hand toward me. I could no longer see Von's face, but I could feel his warmth pulsing through my heart.

A calm resolve came over me. I raised my hand toward his. Our palms touched. A shockwave rippled through my body. He bowed his head slightly. I nodded in reply, then we stepped into the vortex and vanished.

20. Kalisfaar

The positive energy tunnel to Kalisfaar was different than the one I had ridden to Kraegon's world. This one was dark, but had no sparkling lights. It felt smaller in dimension and warmer. I still had the sensation of flying at warp speed, but this time I was going straight down. I kept repeating to myself, *Kalisfaar, Kalisfaar*. I could see Von's glowing Lumen form beside me. His hand clutched mine tightly as we flew through the shaft to the world deep within the Earth's hollow core.

After travelling what seemed just a few minutes, the air mass around us began to shake violently. I gripped Von's hand even tighter, terrified of what might happen if we were to become separated. A painful pressure began building in my ears then a sudden loud popping noise burst us out of the tunnel like a huge snake spitting us from its mouth. My body was thrust through the air. I crashed on the ground then rolled several feet until coming to a stop on my side.

The breath was knocked out of me. I lay on my back until my lungs could fill with air again, then I opened my eyes. The sky was crystal blue with a few white cumulous clouds, just like home. There was a strong, cool breeze.

Dust blew across my face. I raised my hand to shield my eyes.

"Are you okay?" Von asked, standing over me, now back in human form.

"I think so." I was still trying to catch my breath. "Is this Kalisfaar?"

"Yes. Give me your hand."

He helped me stand. I checked to make sure I had my backpack and that Nix and my pendant were still around my neck. I touched the snake's sleek body and felt Athas still entwined in his tail.

"Looks like I made it with all my precious cargo." I stroked Nix gently.

We walked a short distance to Dan, Amara and Kolt. I looked around the landscape of this new world. Red mountains and mesas were in the distance with only a few trees between here and there. Not too far away was a field of giant crystals sticking out of the ground like a forest of glass. The cool wind whipped around us, creating small, spiraling dust devils that zigzagged across the ground. I opened my backpack and took out my jacket.

"What'd you think of that freaky tunnel, sis?" Dan said. "The whole thing blew my mind! I had no idea this other world existed. Imagine how life on Earth would change if more people knew."

"It was pretty crazy. The re-entry was kind of rough." I rubbed my arm and took a swig of water from my water bottle.

"Are you ready to dowse for Oma?" Von asked.

"I was hoping I could use another form of dowsing instead of the map."

"Map dowsing is the only way to find exactly where she is."

Looking for lost animals and people was considered one of the most challenging forms of dowsing, especially if there were emotions involved. How could I map dowse for Oma when even the best dowsers in the world had trouble with it?

I took out the pouch that held the special pendulum and laid the map flat on the ground, stacking rocks on the corners to keep it from blowing away. The pendulum was a pointed crystal with a rounded silver chamber on top. I opened the lid to the chamber carefully and saw a few strands of Oma's white hair inside, then closed it back.

Holding the pendulum by its silver chain over the map, I tried to remember what Oma had taught me. It had been a few years since she had demonstrated how to dowse with a map. I recalled how unbelievably complicated it seemed at the time. Oma's gentle voice came back to me.

"Divide the map into quadrants, then hold the pendulum over each quadrant and ask if your target is there. Continue until you get a yes response then divide that quadrant into smaller spaces and repeat the process. Once you have dowsed the location to a small area, touch the map with your finger while asking the pendulum if this is where your target is. When you get a yes response, you can ask more specific questions concerning that spot."

I tried to ignore everyone as they stood around watching and waiting impatiently once again to see if I would pass or fail the latest dowsing test. Never mind the fact that Oma was out there somewhere, depending on me to get this right.

I began the long process of narrowing the search area down to one spot. When I thought I had found it, I asked the pendulum repeatedly if this were *really* the place where Oma was. The answer was yes each time.

"Okay, I think I have it." I tried to sound confident. The group came closer to look.

"I know where this is," Von said. "It's where the crystal caves are. We can regenerate our energy there. Amara, Dan and Kolt can enter a positive line here and be at the caves in a few minutes. Ysolde and I will have to walk."

"Walk? It looks like it's nearly ten miles to the caves." I looked at the map again.

"We can be there by nightfall. Start dowsing for a line so the others can get to the caves and find Oma."

I began walking around the area feeling for positive energy. I needed to find a line that ran north to the caves. The ground felt hollow and lifeless. After several minutes I returned to the group.

"I can't seem to find anything. Maybe I need to go farther out."

"There should be at least one in this area," Amara said. She walked around us in a large circle then came back with a puzzled look on her face.

"What's wrong?" Von asked.

"I can't feel any energy coming up, either."

"I'll find a line."

We watched as Von walked a half mile, going in a circle that grew wider and wider. I sat down and rubbed Kolt's fur, waiting for him to return. Finally he came back.

"There's nothing. This area is usually full of positive energy from all the crystals. Something's not right."

"Let me ask the pendulum." I unclasped my pendant and asked a few basic questions. "Are there positive energy lines in this area?" The pendulum answered no. "Are there positive energy lines between here and the crystal caves to the northwest?" The pendulum again answered no.

"That's impossible," Amara said. "Your dowsing is ridiculous."

"I'd say it's been working pretty damn well so far, Amara," Dan said, taking up for me. "You need to cut my sister some slack."

I smiled at Dan. "Thanks, bro."

"No problem."

"It appears we'll all have to walk," Von said. "We'll check for energy lines along the way. Of course, Amara, you can stay here if you don't want to walk that far."

"*Whatever*. Let's just go," she said

We headed northwest through the crystal forest toward the mountains. The giant minerals jutted out of the ground in odd angles, casting huge, prismatic reflections onto the red dirt. Dan and I were in awe of the visual spectacle.

I had to walk quickly to keep up with Von's long strides. We stopped periodically so that I could rest a few minutes and check for lines. There was nothing to be found. It was as if all the energy of the land had been consumed.

After many hours, we came to the foothills of the mountains near the caves. There was a narrow worn trail leading up.

"Was that trail made by humans?" I asked Von.

"Kalisfaarians. The Lumen share this northern territory with them. The world within is smaller and more sparsely populated than Earth. Most of the land is surrounded by a vast ocean with a few islands."

"I thought the Lumen had their own world in another dimension like the Vapors."

"We do, but Kalisfaar is our second home."

We trekked up through the foothills. The ground was hard and dry like a desert almost. There were tall, thorny plants that looked like Joshua Trees and spikey green plants with tall stems and white flowers that resembled the yucca plants back home. The sun was beginning to set. The sky was blue-violet with a touch of rose on the horizon. I glanced back and saw three moons rising side-by-side. The center moon was larger than the other two. I wondered how there could even be a sun and three moons inside the Earth.

"Look!" I pointed toward the caves up ahead.

We climbed over rocks to the entrance of the nearest cave. I unclasped my pendant and asked if this was where Oma was. The pendulum responded with no. I asked if we were near the cave she was in. Another no. "Is Oma in *any* of the caves in these mountains?" Again the answer was no. The pendulum had been so sure Oma was here in these caves in this very spot.

I turned to the group. "I'm sorry. I'll try again."

"So we came all this way for nothing?" Amara said to me. "How did you ever become the Domina Lumen?"

"My emotions must have interfered with the results."

"That's enough, Amara," scolded Von. "Negative energy is coming from the cave. Vapors have been here. Ysolde, ask if Oma *was* here."

I asked if Oma had been in this cave recently. The pendulum answered yes. My heart brightened. "Was she here today?" Another yes. "Did she leave alone?" The pendulum gave a no response. "Did she want to leave?" Again, the answer was a definite no.

"Let's go inside. Maybe she left something that would give us a clue," said Dan.

We walked through the opening. The ceiling was high enough so no one had to stoop. The interior was dimly lit. I dug into my backpack for a match and lit it. The tiny flame created a soft glow allowing us to see a sleeping bag and a burned out campfire. A long object lay beside the sleeping bag in the dirt. I lit another match to look closer. It was Oma's wooden cane. My heart sank.

"Oh no," I said softly.

"What?" asked Dan.

"Look." I handed the cane to him.

"She never goes anywhere without this."

"Ysolde, why don't you body dowse to see if Oma left anything important?" asked Von.

I walked slowly around the cave, hoping to feel some kind of sensation. I felt nothing.

"Your emotions are getting in the way. Try again."

I approached the back of the cave and closed my eyes. My palm began to tingle. I took a step back. The sensation went away. When I stepped forward, the sensation returned. With a lighted match I noticed a small mound of loose dirt on the ground as if something had recently been buried. I removed the soil with my hands until I felt a hard object underneath. With the final layer of dirt brushed away, I pulled out a leather-bound book that appeared quite old.

"I found something."

We hurried toward the cave entrance where there was a little more light to see by. I lifted the cover. Inside, the pages were filled with writing, dates and drawings. "I think this may be Oma's journal."

"I didn't know she kept one," said Dan.

I flipped through the pages to the end and read her last entry out loud.

"The Vapors have taken over. They have destroyed the Great Pendulum. I believe the king is being forced to work with them. I must find a way —"

The entry ended with her pen scrawling across the page haphazardly as if it had fallen out of her hand.

"Looks like she was writing when she was taken," I said.

The thought of someone or thing grabbing my frail grandmother and carrying her off to God knows where was almost too much to bear.

I turned to Von. "I remember Oma mentioning the Great Pendulum once, but I forgot what she had said about it."

His face became serious. "Many years ago, the humans built the giant pendulum to banish the Vapors and prevent them from returning. The crystal rotated continuously, creating a positive energy barrier around this world."

"So now there's nothing to stop the Vapors?"

"Right. We must go to the Great Pendulum and restore it."

"Not until we find Oma."

"We will need your grandmother. She is the only one who knows the secret of how to make the Great Pendulum work."

I gazed outside the cave at the starless night sky and the three moons, wondering where Oma could be. A dark form resembling a huge bird flew across one of the moons in the distance. It was the first creature I'd seen in this world. Kolt began barking aggressively as I watched the creature grow in size heading straight for our cave.

"Get to the back of the cave!" Von shouted.

We all ran to the back wall out of sight. A heavy rhythmic swooping sound approached, then a huge shadow crawled across the wall as the gigantic flying creature passed by. Its immense wings stirred the dust around us. I buried my face in Von's shirt. A few minutes later, it returned, coming from the other direction. It hovered a few minutes outside the opening, then the beating sounds of the wings grew less and less intense until there was silence again.

"What the hell was *that*?" asked Dan.

"Drakenz," said Von.

"As in dragon?" Dan's eyes widened.

"I thought the Drakenz were friends with the Lumen," I said. "Oma said they helped create Athas."

"The stone was created on their island of Shi. They are our friends, but I fear they have been taken over by the Vapors," Von said.

"Maybe they took Oma."

"The one we just saw flew south in the direction of Gath Enay, the land of the human king," said Amara.

"I can try to map dowse to see if Oma is there."

"I'll hold a match so you can see." Dan walked over next to me and lit a match.

I spread the map in the dirt and began dowsing over it with Oma's pendulum.

"It's hard to see. Hold the match closer," I said. Dan moved the match right next to the map.

A strong gust of wind suddenly blew into the cave. We all looked toward the entrance to see if another Drakenz had appeared. When we turned back, the map was in flames.

"Put it out!" I yelled.

Dan hurriedly threw dirt on the flames, smothering the fire, but it was too late. The center of the map was destroyed. Only a blackened hole remained.

"Way to go," I said with a heavy sigh. "Now what will we do?"

"Don't blame me! *You* wanted the damn match closer."

"It was an accident. No one's fault," said Von.

"Now we'll have to walk *all over creation* looking for your grandmother while Drakenz hunt us from above." Amara threw her hands in the air.

"Before the map burned, the pendulum showed Oma to be south in the Gath Enay area," I said. "At least we know which direction to go."

"But how will we travel without the Drakenz seeing us?" Dan asked. "Those things are huge!"

"The Drakenz have poor nocturnal vision. I doubt if we see any more of them this evening. Night will be our cloak of safety," said Von.

I felt extremely tired all of a sudden. All the stress was catching up with me. I hadn't eaten anything substantial since we left Oma's Burrow. I knew we had to find Oma, but all I wanted to do was sleep.

"I'm so tired. I don't think I could walk fifty feet right now." I lay down on Oma's sleeping bag. It felt soft with a faint scent of rosemary.

"Von, didn't you say we could regenerate here in the caves?" asked Dan. "Maybe we should do that and let Ysolde rest before we try to cross any more land on foot. She *is* human, after all." He turned toward me. "No offense, sis."

"None taken," I yawned.

"We can spend a few hours regenerating, but if we rest all night, we won't be able to travel safely again until tomorrow night. By then, we may be too late," said Von.

"A few hours' sleep would be heavenly," I mumbled. I snuggled into the downy material and closed my eyes.

"There are no crystals in this cave. We'll have to go to another cave nearby to feed. Ysolde can bring the sleeping bag and sleep in the other cave."

I felt myself transitioning into a dream state. Von's words sounded muffled and unimportant. My body's needs had taken over. My brain was no longer in charge.

"You go without me," I mumbled. The words barely escaped my mouth before I felt myself pass into a deep sleep.

21. Domina Lumen

In my dream, I was back at the canyon hiking down the trail with my family. I could hear the sounds of falcons' voices rising and falling in the distance. Nothing but happiness filled my mind that morning as we headed toward the rim to watch the sun rise and to perform the annual ritual.

I held Oma's hand as we walked along the path through the pinion pines. My mother and father were ahead of us. Mom looked back at me and smiled, then the lavender morning sky turned dark and an ominous shadow appeared above us. I saw a look of terror in Oma's eyes. Kraegon!

I woke with a jolt. When I opened my eyes, I saw three men standing above me. I jerked my body out of the sleeping bag and stumbled to the back of the cave. Von, Dan and the others were gone. Nix and Athas were still around my neck, but I was alone to fend for myself.

The men stood staring at me with great round eyes. They were shorter than I was by at least a foot and dressed simply in what appeared to be peasant clothing. Their pants and coats were natural earth tones. Each one wore boots that came to their knees. They carried medieval weapons.

"Who are you?" I asked.

No one answered. The men talked quietly among themselves then the one with a long white beard and wooden staff stepped forward.

"Are you the Domina Lumen?" he asked. His voice was confident as if he already knew the answer.

I didn't know what to say. What if these men worked for Kraegon?

"Do you serve the king?" I asked. Von had said humans lived south of here in Gath Enay where the king presided. I assumed if these men worked for the king they might be under the influence of Kraegon and had come for me.

"We serve no one," laughed the one with bushy red hair and a beard that almost touched the ground. His big, round belly strained the wooden buttons holding his shirt together. A bow and quiver full of arrows was strapped to his back.

"I am called Ysolde."

"Oh? We were told you were the Domina Lumen," said the one with black hair pulled back in a ponytail. His face was serious. His arms and chest bulged with muscles. A two-handed sword was at his side.

"We've been guarding you for your friends. I am Maedoc the Red," said the one with red hair. "This is Gaufrid the Strong." He pointed to the one with the sword.

"And I am Otho the Elder," said the one with the staff.

The odd little men stood shoulder-to-shoulder, proudly smiling at me.

"So you know my friends?"

"Yes, yes," said Otho.

"Two men, a lady and a white wolf?"

"Yes, those are the ones." Otho smiled.

"Where are they?"

"We are here to take you to them. Now, gather your things and follow us."

"How do I know I can trust you?"

"Ah, I almost forgot." Otho dug in his pocket and pulled out a folded piece of paper and handed it to me.

It was the remnants of the burned map with a note scrawled on the back. I read the note quietly to myself.

"Ysolde, you can trust these guys. Remember the vinegar. – Dan."

Dan's overdosing on vinegar when he was a kid was becoming our secret code, it seemed. I looked at the three little men. They seemed friendly enough.

"All right, I'll go with you. Is it far where we're going?"

"Not too far. You'll see," Maedoc said.

I rolled up Oma's sleeping bag and put her journal inside my backpack, then picked up her cane and walked toward the entrance to the cave.

"My friends and I were supposed to leave last night to find Oma. We should've been in Gath Enay by now. Are we going there?"

Maedoc chuckled, "No, lass. We're going to our home in the Crystal Mountains here in Kalisfaar."

Otho noticed Oma's cane. He ran his fingers gently up and down the wood, admiring the carvings.

"That belonged to your grandmother, did it not?" he asked.

"Do you know my grandmother Oma? Is she okay?" My heart beat quickened.

"We don't know her by *that* name. We know her as the elder Domina Lumen. We believe she's being held captive in the tower at Serpent Lake."

"Serpent Lake? If we know where she is, we should leave at once!"

"All in good time, lass. First we must get you safely to your friends," Maedoc said.

"Yes, yes. Now come along." Otho put his hand on my back and gently guided me out of the cave and onto a nearby trail.

I followed the men through the winding, narrow passageways of the red foothills. They scurried along the steep trails with the sure-footedness of mountain goats. I struggled to keep up. Finally, after what seemed at least an hour, we came to a large opening in the side of a mountain where many little people were milling around inside and out.

"What is this place?"

"This is our home," said Otho. "Come. Your friends await you."

We walked past guards dressed in armor holding spear-like weapons. Archers were stationed on a rock ledge above. Two massive iron gates opened as we approached. After passing through the gates, we came upon two thick wooden fortress doors. Beyond the wooden doors was an enormous room filled with blacksmiths, tailors, armorers, bakers, alchemists and a market with fresh food. My mouth watered as we passed a stack of freshly baked bread.

Maedoc grabbed a large loaf and tore off a hunk, stuffing it into his mouth. "It's made with mead and herbs," he chuckled.

"You look hungry," Otho said with a warm smile. He handed me a small, dark loaf.

I took a bite. The soft texture melted in my mouth with an earthy, sweet taste, reminding me of Oma's home-baked rosemary bread.

"Follow me," said Otho.

We walked along a lengthy hallway with many doors on either side. Halfway down, Otho stopped in front of a door that had crystals embedded into the wood. When he opened it, Dan, Amara and Kolt were standing on the other side.

"Hey sis! You finally made it! We were getting worried." Dan grabbed me with a reassuring hug. His arms enveloped my body like a warm security blanket.

"What a relief it is to see you!" I said to him.

Kolt ran to my side. I knelt beside him and stroked his muzzle. He licked my face and sniffed my hair.

"Where's Von?" I asked, wishing he'd been there to greet me.

"He's making arrangements for our departure to Gath Enay," Amara said. "We need to wait for nightfall again before we can leave."

"We were supposed to leave last night. Why didn't you guys wake me?"

"Otho and his men showed up soon after you fell asleep," Dan said. "They said they'd guard you. You were so tired; we decided to let you sleep while we regenerated in the crystal cave. You slept all night and most of today."

"Otho said Oma is in a tower at Serpent Lake," I said.

"Yes," Amara said. "We'll be leaving in a few hours and should be at the tower before dawn."

"You have time to eat and bathe," Otho said to me. "Please, make yourself at home."

I sat down in one of the ornately carved chairs placed along the walls of the room. Hand-woven tapestries of strange creatures, kings, queens and knights hung from the ceiling. At the end of the room a large tapestry of a woman covered most of the wall. The woman was dressed in a white gown standing next to a spring of water coming out of the ground. A snake was coiled around her neck and she was holding a black rock. Chills ran though my body. I walked over to the tapestry to examine it closer.

"The lady in the tapestry is Kespara," said Gaufrid. "She was the original Domina Lumen, your great ancestor."

I thought about the day in the Burrow when Oma told me the history of the stone and the Domina Lumen.

"I remember Oma telling me about her."

"You are descended from great and powerful women," Otho said.

Apparently I didn't inherit those great powers. If I were really great and powerful, we would have Oma here safely with us and all would be well. Unfortunately, her life was in my hands.

"Are you coming with us to Gath Enay? We'll need a guide."

"Maedoc and Gaufrid will lead the way. I am too old to go into the wilds. I will try to be of use to you by working my magick from here."

"Are you a wizard?" I asked.

"Otho is the wisest of them all," Maedoc said.

I looked at Dan. "Wow, can you believe this? A real wizard!"

"I know, right? This is so cool, except for all the bad stuff, of course."

How often does a person get to meet a real wizard? I wanted to pick his brain and learn how to zap things and do all that wizards do, but there wasn't time.

"What about the Drakenz?" Dan asked.

"You mean the Inquiry?" said Otho.

I looked at the others and no one seemed to know what he was talking about.

"The Inquiry was recently created by Kraegon. It is a select group of humans who have been persuaded to work with the Vapors. They ride the Drakenz searching for criminals, suspicious characters and dowsers."

237

"What? Dowsers?"

I put my hand on my crystal pendant and felt a slight vibration in my palm as if the crystal was acknowledging my shock and concern. I knew I was the target for being the Domina Lumen, but dowsers hadn't been persecuted for centuries on Earth. Of course, this wasn't Earth.

"You heard me correctly," Otho said. "When Kraegon and the Vapors took control of the lands, they took control of everything, including all the fresh water and underground springs. No one is allowed to dowse for water or even directions. If you're caught using a pendulum, a rod or any dowsing instrument for any reason, you will be arrested."

"But how will we find Oma without my dowsing?"

He touched my crystal pendant and looked me in the eye. "You will need to be very careful. Disguise your dowsing, if you can."

"In other words, you'll need to body dowse as much as possible and we all know how *that* goes," Amara said.

"Maybe you'd like to give it a try if you think it's that easy," I replied, wishing Amara would give me a little credit for all the things I actually had accomplished on this hideous journey. She remained silent.

Otho opened the door. "Come, I will show you to a private room for your bath and fresh clothes."

I followed him a short distance down the hall to a smaller room that had a simple bed, chair, table and a round wooden tub with a tent-like cloth on top.

"Someone will bring you food and fill the tub shortly."

Otho left the room. I set my backpack on the table and took my jacket off. It was almost impossible to relax knowing we would be leaving this safe haven soon, heading into extreme danger in the land Otho called "the wilds."

A gentle knock came upon the door. Two petite women entered, smiling.

"Lady Domina, we brought you some food and warm water for your bath."

Lady Domina? I liked the sound of that. I suddenly felt quite regal in my filthy jeans and rat nest hair. The women put a full basket of food on the table then poured two pails of steaming water into the tub.

"It's not a lot of water, my lady. But it's enough for a quick bath," said one of the women. Another woman entered the room carrying some clothes.

"I hope you don't mind, my lady, but we thought you might want to change so you would look more like one of us. You'll be safer."

She laid out a pair of dark trousers, a white blouse, underthings, a belt, a thick gray scarf, gloves and a long overcoat with a hood.

"I guessed at your size. I hope these fit properly." She set a brand new pair of brown riding boots on the floor.

"Thank you for your kindness," I said.

The little women curtsied and left the room, closing the door behind them.

I stripped down and stepped into the tub. The water felt too hot at first, but soon my body adjusted as I eased into the steam. The women had placed rose petals on top of the water. They gave the air an uplifting, sweet fragrance like Mom's rose garden right after a summer rain. I closed my eyes and breathed the scent in deeply.

Mom's smiling face suddenly flashed before me then disappeared. I missed home. The life of Ysolde Hartmaan had been taken over completely by Domina Lumen. I had no idea how to be Domina Lumen. I wasn't a regal, mystical figure like Kespara. In my heart, I was just a small-town girl from Texas.

After the bath, I dried off and tried on the clothes. They had a faint scent of wood smoke, reminding me of the way Cam smelled the day he helped me move in to the dorm another life time ago.

The clothes fit well. I buttoned the blouse and left it hanging out then tucked the pants into the boots and tried on the overcoat. I tied the wool scarf around my neck in a way that would hide Nix, Athas and my crystal pendent from the Inquiry. My image in the mirror was a medieval fantasy come true. I wasn't wearing armor, but Furia would still be proud. The happy feeling was fleeting though, as the gravity of what I was about to do set in.

On the floor beside my pack was a new brown satchel that one of the women must have left for me. It was much larger than my backpack and had many compartments. I placed my entire backpack with all its precious contents inside.

"Perfect," I said.

The food basket contained breads, cheeses, nuts, fruits and a generous flask of water with a strap that made it handy for carrying. I made a cheese sandwich and ate it quickly, then stuffed the rest of the food into the various compartments of the new pack. I flung the water flask over one shoulder and the satchel over the other then left the room to join the others. They met me in the hall. Everyone was dressed in medieval peasant clothing.

"Aren't we a merry band," Dan chuckled.

"Our video game is becoming a bit too real," I said, feeling my stomach tighten into knots as our time of departure approached.

"They gave you a spiked mace for a weapon."

Dan handed the iron, bat-like weapon to me. Attached to the end was an iron ball covered with long, sharp points. I touched one of them. A small drop of blood oozed from my finger tip.

Furia had wielded a mace in the game, so I knew how the weapon worked in theory, but I had never actually used one before. I wasn't thrilled with another melee weapon where I'd have to get close to my opponent to hit him. A bow would have been much better.

"What's your weapon?" I asked Dan.

"A flail."

He held up a long, cylindrical iron weapon with a spiked ball and chain attached to the end.

"Apparently, I don't rank getting a sword."

"Normally, the Lumen wouldn't be using these clunky weapons at all," Amara scoffed, repositioning a handsome recurve bow and quill on her shoulder. "But with the positive energy blocked from this planet, we can't use our energy shards."

"I'll be glad to trade if you don't like that bow," I said, holding my mace toward her.

"I don't do melee," she replied offhandedly.

"No surprise there," Dan grinned. "We all have daggers, just in case something gets close and personal."

He placed one inside the sheath attached to my belt.

"Even you, Amara." He handed a dagger to her. She waved him away.

"Enough about these ridiculous, archaic weapons! Von is waiting for us outside."

Dan ignored Amara and thrust a dagger into the sheath on her belt. "You'll thank me for that someday."

Maedoc led us through the hall to a side exit out of the mountain. The sun had set. Gray clouds hung low overhead, covering the three moons from view. The early evening air was crisp and chilly. The scent of snow was in the air.

We walked to a circular corral with horses saddled and waiting. Von was standing next to a white stallion. His eyes lit up when he saw me. All of his warmth embraced my heart. I smiled back as I walked over to him. He looked handsome in his long black overcoat and black boots. His hair was pulled back in a ponytail and he carried a two handed sword.

"You look rested," he said, gently touching my cheek. Goosebumps ran up and down my arms as his energy pulsed across my skin. I wanted to tell him how much I cared about him, but not in front of the others. Life was serious now. There was no time for romance, even though my heart said otherwise.

"I'm nervous, especially not being able to dowse openly with my pendulum."

"We'll find a way. I have something for you." He handed me a rolled up scroll. I opened it.

"A new map!"

"Promise me, no matches near this one?"

"I promise. Thank you for having this made."

"It was no problem. Are you ready to continue our quest?"

"I don't think it matters if I'm ready or not. Oma needs us."

I stroked the mane of the stallion. The white horse turned his head toward me and nuzzled my arm with his nose just like my horse Rio used to do. Rio was a massive black Appaloosa with dappled white spots on his rump. At seventeen hands tall, most folks thought he was too big for me, but he was a gentle giant. I rode him bareback through the fields back home. Someone shot him with an arrow one night. I found him the next morning in the pasture, dying. That was my first real encounter with the cruelties of the world.

"I don't know how we can do all of this and survive," I said with a heavy sigh. "How can we travel to Oma without getting caught? If we happen *not* to get caught, how will we rescue her? Cam is still in a crystal, probably dead by now. We have to restore the Great Pendulum. You all have limited powers without your energy shards. You don't have your energy signature. Kraegon has taken over this world and somehow we're supposed to eradicate him? There's no way we can do it all."

"We have to focus on one goal at a time, Ysolde. Maedoc and Gaufrid will guard us to Gath Enay. Getting there safely is our first goal. I will protect you no matter what comes."

Von's crystal blue eyes gazed into mine. I knew he would protect me, but at what cost? I'd almost rather go alone than risk his existence or Dan's again.

Maedoc walked over to us and patted the stallion's chest. The great horse nuzzled his face.

"Moon will be your horse for this journey, my lady. He's strong and brave. You won't find a steadier companion."

"Hello, beautiful Moon."

I gently scratched the side of the stallion's head. His ears perked in my direction.

"Everyone mount up!" exclaimed Gaufrid.

I gathered the reins and put my foot in the stirrup, then pulled myself up into the saddle, which was more like a padded blanket.

It felt good to be on horseback again. The horses had rope nooses around their noses and no bits in their mouths. I admired the Kalisfaarians for their kindness toward the horses. They were treated more like partners than beasts of burden.

Gaufrid rode his small black stallion out of the corral. We followed him single file on a narrow path down the mountain heading south.

Von was in front of me on a large bay stallion. Dan was behind on a buckskin with Amara following on a pretty gray mare. Maedoc brought up the rear riding another small black stallion. Kolt trotted alongside Von.

The wind was steady and frigid. Snow began falling. It stuck to my eyelashes and Moon's mane like tiny tufts of cotton candy. I raised my hood and checked my scarf, making sure Nix, Athas and my pendant were still hidden from view.

Von turned and looked back at me. I smiled at him, giving my best impression that all was well. He slowed his horse until Moon caught up and we rode side by side. I felt warm and protected. I didn't think I could live without Von now. He had become such a part of me.

I turned and looked back at Dan. He grinned and gave me a thumbs up. His eyes were sparkling with excitement.

The role of Domina Lumen was becoming etched into my soul. I could see the image of Kespara holding the stone and felt her presence riding along with me. I wasn't just anyone anymore. This was all real. Despite the danger, I knew I was right where I was meant to be. I patted Moon on the withers, took a deep breath and settled in for the long journey ahead.

The End

About the Author

M.E Neidhardt is an artist, writer, dowser and casual online fantasy gamer where she routinely gets thrashed in pvp (player vs. player). She graduated from Austin College and has lived in several places, including France, where she studied art. She met the hawk in chapter one while living in a tent at Arcosanti in Arizona. She shares her tiny house in Texas with her rescued, four-legged friends and hikes in Colorado whenever she gets the chance.

Visit her at: meneidhardt.com

Dear reader,

Thank you for reading my first novel. If you are interested in learning more about dowsing, seek out the American Society of Dowsers online. The inspiration for the location of this book came from the Black Canyon of the Gunnison in Colorado. If you enjoyed this story and could give a little feedback on Amazon, Goodreads or elsewhere, I would greatly appreciate the support.

Embrace the energy! ~ M.E. Neidhardt